D0226825

BED OF STRINGS

NINE STORIES

© 2021

All Rights Reserved

ISBN: 978-1-6671-4269-2
Imprint: Lulu.com

First Edition – September 2021

Contents

Forward

One of the joys I've found in writing is the naming of stories. Titling is not so much a process as it is an inspiration, which comes when it comes. A writer's inspiration … a writer's *Muse* … appears briefly, attracted by toil alone, and only when she is needed. Never when she is wanted.

A title then is an inspired distillation to a few words of what a story, or a book, is about … a peek, meant to intrigue. So, what is *A Bed of Strings?* Simply this - nine stories with woven themes … strings … touching on death, illness, divorce, insecurity, and suicide. Grim, yes? But the stories are balanced with strength of will, redemption, humor, love, and humanity.

The strings resonate, like chords played on a mandolin, to create a bed … a bed of strings, leading one to dreams of their own.

In writing these tales I did my best to stay out of their way, and my wish is you'll enjoy getting lost in them. My aim is to entertain and to provoke some, but not too much, thought.

If you find the stories gritty, I blame *Calliope*, chief of muses. It was she who made me do it. I was, in fact, powerless to not bring them forth.

Lee Forbes - Saint Petersburg, Florida.

Dec. 25th, in the dreadful, and wonderful, year of 2020.

Dedicated to the special few who helped me find my voice. You know who you are.

Thank you!

... lay down your weary tune, lay down.

Lay down the song you strum,

and rest yourself

beneath the strength of strings,

that no voice can hope to hum.

\- Bob Dylan

... and we'll blow away forever soon,
and go on to different lands.

And please do not ever look for me,

but with me you will stay,

and you will hear yourself in song,

blowing by one day.

\- Suzanne Vega

The Harvest

In 1972 there was a lot going on in the world and, as a miserable high school sophomore, I was aware of some of it. It didn't seem like it then, but it was a time of contrasts … highs and lows, in a lockstep of awful and wonderful. The war in Vietnam was winding down, but peace demonstrations raged across America. Nixon was executing peerless foreign diplomacy while visiting Beijing and Moscow, but his burglars were arrested at The Watergate. Terrorists were killing Israeli Olympians in Munich, while the Pioneer 10 spacecraft beamed close-up photos of Jupiter and her moons back to Houston.

In popular culture, *Gunsmoke* was still in the top 10 TV shows nationally, but it was being beat out in the ratings by *All in the Family* and *Sanford and Son.*

Gilbert O'Sullivan and Melanie were in the top 10 A.M. radio hits, while Led Zeppelin released *Stairway to Heaven,* and Blue Oyster Cult released their first album.

Cassette tapes were battling with vinyl LP's and 8-track tapes for the premier format in music, while Steve Jobs and

Steve Wozniak sold their first illegal *blue boxes* - the creation of Apple was still four years off.

The future was ripping itself from the past in 1972 and I was in the middle of it all. I hadn't heard Led Zeppelin yet, but I remember thinking Creedence Clearwater on our 12-pound *portable* cassette player was the height of human achievement. And so it was for me - 1972 - the backdrop of my youth.

High school sophomores in all places and times deserve pity, but I was a particularly woeful specimen. My name is Paul. My parents divorced when I was eleven and my younger brother Mac and I stayed with our mom. Our dad had custody of us on alternating weekends, and sometimes he even picked us up.

Mac and I dealt with our parents' divorce in our own ways; he by befriending the Mormon kids in the neighborhood, and I by choosing juvenile delinquency. Mom took the only decent-paying job she could find, which was on the graveyard shift. She was a supervisor at a regional bank, in their data processing center, overseeing staff handling tens of thousands of paper checks overnight. The upshot of this was a remarkably unsupervised adolescence for me.

With chipped front teeth from a playground accident in the fourth grade, not many friends, and no understanding of what I was doing in the world, I was a poster boy for a lonely underachiever. I sometimes wonder now if I'd grown up in the 2000s, would I have been another Dylan Klebold, going to school one day to gun down a few dozen of my closest enemies. But, as fortune would have it, I found myself in this dark place in the 70s instead. I fell in with a small assortment of other kids who were delinquents like myself and engaged in a string of petty crimes for which I was never held accountable, except by Karma. How I didn't get caught shoplifting, smoking pot, stealing bicycles, breaking into garages, and even a house once, I will never know.

One episode which haunts me still happened one afternoon when I was hanging out with Donny, the most criminal of my few friends. We were at my house and were throwing darts at the garage door (they were wood doors back then). We got bored and were standing near the sidewalk when we saw a kid, about 7 or 8 years old, riding a bike across the street about 75 yards away.

The boy was unaware of us, and Donny said,

"I'll bet I can nail that kid with this dart."

I looked and judged the distance impossible.

"There's no frigging way you could hit him from here, dude. Don't even try."

I should have known better. Donny stabilized himself, spreading his feet apart. He arched backward, the hand with the dart almost touching the ground, and with a mighty heave he let the dart fly. It took a moment for my eyes to catch sight of it, arcing across a cloudless sky, lifting for an enormous distance, and I watched it fall back to earth. In a moment I realized with horror the dart had pinned itself in the kid's skull.

The boy stopped in the middle of the street in mid-pedal, and we could see him, feet spread to hold his bike up, one hand holding his handlebar, the other hand reaching up to his head, frantically feeling the dart. He didn't pull it out but felt it all over for what seemed an eternity.

The boy, in a clear panic, rode off at the fastest pace he could manage, with the dart sticking out of his head, still unaware of who his assailants were.

I'd have to do a lot of hard thinking to recall how many years went by before I was ever again equally sickened, but it was a lot of them.

I didn't hang around with Donny much afterward. It wasn't because I thought I was better than him, but because I thought I was as bad as him, and it shamed me, and I became even more of a loner. There wasn't a shred of self-esteem for anyone to find in me and I preferred being alone, not explaining

4

anything about myself to anyone, not that I felt there was anyone who cared enough to ask. To my fortune, it turned out I was wrong about that part.

I had a remarkable record of truancy from school by this time, and it got worse. What was odd about my ditching school was I spent almost all my time at the public library. Days and weeks reading and studying topics of interest to me, reading books of history and geography, and on insects and architecture, and more than a little science fiction. This was life for me until *the harvest*.

There is a saying - *Every dog has his day* - and I always took it to mean no matter how down and out someone is, there's always a chance of something amazing happening to change their circumstance. My chance came in the second week of September that year.

School was back in session for only a few weeks, and I hated it already. One early evening, my dad stopped by our house. My parents were split for about three years by now and were on civil terms. Mom let dad into the house, and we stood in the living room. He got straight to the point.

"Something's come up and I need to talk with you both."

He didn't look distressed, but he was serious. We sat down around the dining table, and he continued.

5

"My brother Henry is in the hospital from a pretty serious heart attack. He's undergone a triple bypass surgery and won't be able to get his harvest in this year."

I knew Uncle Henry and his family from two visits they made to us in California over the past few years, and from a memorable trip our family made to Illinois to see them on their farm. We stayed there for a few weeks when I was in junior high and for Mac and me, it was the best vacation ever. We loved the wide-open spaces, all the farm animals, the amazing farmhouse meals, flirting with girls at the city pool during the week, and in church on Sundays, and mostly we enjoyed being kids with our four cousins.

Dad went on explaining what was happening.

"His entire crop of corn and soybeans is at risk, and it could ruin them financially if it isn't brought in, and soon."

Mom, looking concerned, asked what they were going to do.

"Well, I've been on the phone with Henry, and we've got an idea. I want to take Paul and Jake with me, and we're going to drive to Illinois and do the harvest."

Jake was another cousin from my dad's sister. He was about six years older than me, and I idolized him.

Dad continued.

"It will keep Paul out of school for about four weeks and so I'll need to get with his teachers and gather assignments and keep him on track in the evenings, if you agree."

I was, of course, in favor of this whole idea and I wasted no time saying so. Looking back, I believe Mom was relieved. If anyone ever needed a break from raising a sullen teen, she was the one. She didn't speak at first but looked at me long.

"Well, it will help their family and the experience will be good for Paul, so yes, he can go."

And just that fast, she signed off on my grand adventure and an escape from my miserable existence, at least for a while.

Dad and Jake had grown close a few years before when dad helped him get through some legal troubles. Jake had dodged the draft for Vietnam, and he left home to avoid arrest, traveling the country. Jake was gone for over a year, going as far as Canada for a short time, but he came back home eventually, and paid the price to Uncle Sam.

I never learned the details, but I knew Dad helped him with a lawyer and gave him a place to live after his 18-months at a low-risk federal pen in Lompoc. Dad told us he and Jake talked, and he'd jumped at the chance to go.

Dad left shortly after securing mom's agreement, saying he'd be back to pick me up in the morning, after coordinating my absence with my school.

The next morning, I was up early, and ready. It was a school day, and I was happy already not to be sitting in a classroom ... or ditching class. Mom was home from her job and, rather than go to bed, she stayed up to see me off. She was in a good mood and busied herself with making breakfast, then employing me to help her with dishes. She talked with me about it being a good thing I was doing and urged me to use the experience to think about what I wanted to do with my life, what I wanted to do for work when I was older. Dishes now done, we were sitting in the living room, talking, and waiting for dad, while Creedence was wailing *Looking Out My Backdoor* on the cassette deck.

"You have to keep up in school while on this trip, Paul. Your future depends on it."

Unconvinced, I assured her I would.

I heard Dad's truck roll up the driveway right then. I gathered my gear and headed for the door. Taking a last look around, I listened to the strains of *Up Around the Bend* filling the room, and then finally looked at mom. I kissed her cheek in appreciation, and she grabbed my bookbag (which I hoped she wouldn't notice sitting on the floor) and helped me out to the truck.

Approaching Dad's truck, I noticed a new and entirely ugly, yet serviceable, plywood camper shell bolted to the bed. He and Jake got out to greet us and they helped get my gear stowed in the back.

The back bed held a twin mattress, covered with a big goose-down sleeping bag. Jake and Dad's luggage was stuffed along both sides of the mattress, and it looked like a cozy space for a long drive.

"We all three can fit in the cab and Jake and I will be rotating driving every four hours, straight through. We'll all take turns in the truck bed for our sack time when we need sleep. We're stopping for meals and gas only. It'll take us about 32 hours to get there."

With that, we were off. The trip through the Southwest U.S., and into the heartland of America, was an adventure. I enjoyed the captive time with dad and Jake, and the scenery and storms we passed through on the way. The little bit of sack-time I got was enough, and I was not uncomfortable dozing off in the cab either. Dad and Jake talked and told me stories for hours. I was gathering a feeling of belonging. It was the shortest 32 hours of my life.

Right on schedule, we exited the freeway just past Bloomington, Illinois onto a two-lane country road. I was awake to see the first light of morning. It seemed we had sailed for hours through a sea of cornfields when Dad finally turned down a long gravel driveway leading up to Henry's two-story farmhouse.

The driveway split at a sizable front yard and wrapped in a circle around the back. Dad guided the truck around the driveway, and I recognized the barns and corncribs off to the right and the house and gas pump to the left.

An English-Setter came bounding off the back porch and was barking his greetings at us. It was Ruffles! I remembered him from my last visit a few years before, when he was just a tiny pup.

Alerted by Ruffles' barking and the sound of tires on the gravel drive, members of the family came out of the house to meet us. They helped us unload our luggage and get it into the house. I'd never felt so welcome anywhere. My cousin Penny showed me to my room, and to my delight, I was assigned the entire basement. True, it was only half-finished, but had its own bathroom and a big, comfortable bed. I dropped my gear, and we went back upstairs.

The girls were setting the dining table, the biggest I'd ever seen, which could seat 12 people. Uncle Henry and Aunt Julie were asking about our trip and my cousins seemed as excited at our arrival as I was to be there. Henry moved to stand in front of dad, Jake, and me.

"You boys have no idea how glad I am you're here. Welcome! We waited lunch for you. Come sit."

I sat and looked at my extended family.

Shawn, the youngest, was cool. He was the baby of the group, and I was intrigued because he looked and acted so much like Mac and me. He was like another brother, but a bit shy at first.

There was nothing shy about the girls. All three were tall, fierce, and beautiful. What I liked best about them though was that when they talked with me, they looked me in the eye, and listened.

Diane was two years older than me. I enjoyed the subtle, yet constant, tension between her and her mom as much as our talks later about what we were going to do when we left home.

Penny was my age, and we could have been twins. For some reason I trusted her like no one else. She was brutally honest and yet very compassionate, with a razor wit and calm style.

11

Abby, a year younger than I, was a living doll. She was sweet to her core and just radiated positive energy, a *goodness* you could feel, which made you want to be around her.

Lastly, were the folks.

Uncle Henry was gregarious, with a rare adult quality; he made kids laugh and feel important. He was high energy and I saw all the qualities in his kids combined in him.

Aunt Julie was an equally nice, yet intimidating woman. She was a great mom, the type you liked being around, but you knew you'd better not act up or she'd call you out.

Looking around the table, I knew I was a lucky boy and I felt at home immediately.

Henry waited for us to be seated and then led in saying grace. He then spent the rest of the meal talking about his recent adventures getting a triple bypass and how his medications were affecting him.

"I have more prescriptions than you can shake a stick at and hell, one of them is making me pee in Technicolor!"

This brought on a round of snickering from us kids, and a stern look from Julie.

"No kidding, my pee is the brightest, glow-in-the-dark shade of orange you ever saw."

Julie could take no more.

"Please Henry! Not at the table."

Henry looked to Julie and the kids with a smile. He stopped talking for the moment while we laughed even more. Dad brought the subject around to the plan for the harvest and Henry outlined how he thought it should go.

"The soybean fields need to be done first, then the corn. We've got 1,080 acres in total. I'm thinking Jake can run the combine and Darrin (my dad), you can run the grain trailers to the elevators in town. Paul, you'll drive the International and do all the chisel plowing of the fields after Jake has run the combine through them. That'll get them ready for our next spring planting."

We listened, knowing how important the plan was for the family, and I realized with excitement I was going to be running a full-sized tractor on a real farm. Henry continued.

"Depending on the weather, it'll take somewhere between three and four weeks to finish. Again, I'm grateful to the Lord you boys are here."

Henry said he was feeling good enough to walk out to the barn and show us how to operate all the equipment and where to find everything we would need. On the way to the barn, I felt Dad's hand rest on my shoulder as we walked, something he hadn't done for years. I almost flinched, then I just enjoyed it.

Every day seemed it was the best of my life up to then. They were ordinary days, each filled with small experiences, and I felt a growing sense of belonging. It was what I craved since my parents divorced, without knowing what *it* was, but I was getting an inkling …

It was being around a big family, learning to drive a tractor, and walks along quiet country roads in a sea of standing corn taller than me.

It was going to Kmart for high-top work boots, making friends with barnyard cats, and leading grace for the first time at dinner.

It was having the entire basement as a bedroom to myself, making cookies with my aunt, and standing on the porch during hellacious thunder and lightning storms.

It was farm-cooked meals, seeing a huge hunter's moon touching the earth, and being proud when standing in a store with my cousins.

It was ordinary … which for me was extraordinary. I felt sadness and doubt leaving my soul, and I welcomed their departure.

Of the many highlights on that trip, there were three experiences which were key in changing the direction of my life.

The first was a simple conversation with my dad. We were sitting one evening while he reviewed my progress on my homework, and after looking it over, he leaned back and talked with me, like an adult. He said he was proud of the work I was doing. It was unusual for him to offer praise and I soaked it up like rain in a desert. While we talked, he became thoughtful for a moment, and sighed heavily.

"One of the few things I regret in my life son is the pain you, your brother, and your mom felt when we divorced. I'd give about anything to take it back, but I can't … I just want you to know I am really sorry."

It was a rare thing, an apology from him. Our relationship began to heal after that.

The other two experiences involved Uncle Henry. They had the feel of casual lessons, but in the long term, they changed everything for me.

One afternoon, as the clan was finishing lunch, Diane announced she had somewhere to go and, car keys in hand, she left through the back door. The rest of us were pitching in, clearing the table, when Diane burst back into the house, less than a minute after leaving, and she was screaming for her dad.

15

Bursting into tears she told him she started to drive away and heard a loud yelp of pain and stopped. She didn't know Ruffles had been laying in the shade under the car.

"Papa, I ran over Ruffles, and he's hurt bad," she said, sobbing deeply.

The other cousins and I ran out to the driveway and saw Ruffles laying there, with his lower body crushed, whimpering in agony. After less than a minute, Henry calmly emerged from the farmhouse with a pistol in his hand. The cylinder of the gun was open, and he was dropping a single bullet shell into one of the chambers.

"You kids go on inside now."

It was clear he was going to end Ruffles' life, and my cousins sobbed as they retreated to the farmhouse. I was sad but composed. Henry looked me up and down.

"You should stay and watch, if you will."

Meeting his eyes, I nodded affirmatively. Henry closed the cylinder and knelt to Ruffles, putting a gentle hand to his head, petting him.

"I'm so sorry boy. Be at peace now."

Henry pointed the gun at Ruffles' head, out of the dog's line of sight I noticed, and without delay he fired, ending Ruffle's life.

I knew what was going to happen before it did, but I flinched when the gun went off anyway. Ruffles' body jerked once when struck by the bullet, and he moved no more.

I felt nauseous, and the smell of cordite hung between us in the air. Henry, keeping the barrel of the pistol pointed at the ground, double-checked the cylinder, making sure it was empty, then put the pistol in his pocket. He looked to Ruffles, sighed, and then looked to me.

"Come to the barn with me. We've got to get some things to bury him."

Before turning to follow, I looked toward the farmhouse and saw my dad looking out the window at his brother and I. He met my gaze and nodded in Henry's direction, as if urging me to follow him.

I did.

I was in the barn, trying to grasp the finality of what I had just seen, when Henry began to speak.

"It's a sad, sad thing son, but a fact of life. I asked you to stay because I don't imagine you see many animals put out of their misery in the city, and there are a lot of important lessons about life out here."

Henry pulled a folded burlap bag from a shelf as he talked, then headed toward a rack of hand tools hanging on the barn wall.

"Your cousin Shawn is a bit too young for this just yet, but there will be other animals, and that's the point I guess … death happens to us all."

He selected two shovels from the wall, hanging from nails. Handing me one and grabbing the other for himself, he continued.

"As a man in this world, you will have to make many hard decisions and perform many grim tasks, like this one. Out here on the farm you need to know if an injured or sick animal is going to live or not if you can connect them to a vet who's hours away. If the animal can't make it, then the only mercy you can show is to end their pain."

Henry motioned me to follow, and we walked with the shovels and the bag back to where Ruffles lay. Henry knelt, slowly and gently easing Ruffles' body into the bag. He then cradled him in his arms. Henry carried Ruffles and I followed with the two shovels. We walked across the large back yard and stopped under a very large oak tree by the white rail fence defining the edge of the yard from the corn field beyond.

Without being asked, I started digging a grave about six feet from the base of the tree. After about 30 minutes, we managed a suitable hole of about three feet by three feet, and five feet deep. Henry shaped the edges of the grave from above, while I cleared the middle. When we were finished, I reached up to set my shovel aside on the lawn and motioned Henry to hand Ruffles down to me. He looked at me with a bit of surprise and, kneeling, he handed Ruffles down to me.

It was a tight fit, but I could crouch just enough to lay Ruffles gently in the center of his resting place, and I smoothed our furry friend's shroud, and said goodbye.

"So long little buddy. I'm going to miss you."

I climbed out of the grave, carful to not step on Ruffles.

Henry looked to the farmhouse and whistled loudly.

"Kids, come now, so we can lay Ruffles to rest."

A new round of sobbing could be heard from the back porch, and everyone walked over and joined us. The mood was somber as we formed a circle around Ruffles in the breezy shade of the trees. Henry knew just what to say.

"We all here are upset because our friend, Ruffles, was taken from us before we expected, and in a shocking way. We are going to miss him for sure. Diane, honey, don't believe you are to blame. God works in mysterious ways, and it was Ruffles'

19

time to go. He's in a better place now, and we will all, someday, be there with him again."

This brought on another round of sobbing, but more peaceful than before. After a silence, Henry and I took up the shovels and began covering the grave.

The family began to drift away from the circle, one by one, until only Henry and I remained. When the grave was filled, we stood quietly. I stirred first and began walking to the barn. Henry followed and continued his line of thought as we walked.

"Life is sad son. Without an absolute faith there is something better for us at the end of life, it is so sad and frightening that it isn't even bearable for most people."

The barn was dim and cool as we entered and reset the shovels on their nail hangers.

"As a man, and a father someday yourself, you'll do well to take note of what you saw today. Ending Ruffles' life was hard, but it wasn't the most important thing to happen. What matters most in death and tragedy is looking after those of us left behind. When you're grown, your main job will be to bring strength, peace of mind, and protection to your family."

As I laid down to go to sleep later, I thought about everything I'd seen, and compared it to my life in California.

Man ... this is intense! They sure as hell don't teach this kind of thing at Redondo High.

I wasn't used to being talked to like an adult, and I liked it, but I was also shocked by what he'd done. He was awesome, but I also now feared him ... just a little. This conflicting view I had of him remained with me until several days later when I saw him in yet another light, and he provided the third experience which changed my direction.

We were into the first week of October and progress on the harvest was ahead of schedule. At supper, Henry told us he made a commitment to a charity event several months earlier.

"It's a sponsored walk for hunger relief. I am on the board of a group called CROP, and we do activities to help feed poor people around the world. Tomorrow is our annual *Walk for Hunger.* Henry, smiling mischievously, told us the rest.

"My doctor cleared me yesterday to participate and, you didn't know it until now, but the three of you volunteered to walk in my place the day you got here. I must stay in the starting - line canopy and I'm allowed to walk only one mile. I took the liberty of lining up all your sponsors."

The next evening, we rolled into the parking lot of the University of Illinois, up in Bloomington, and we made our way to the gathering place for the walk. There were several hundred

21

people there and Henry went about getting us signed in and introducing us to people he knew there, which seemed to be almost all of them.

It became clear from the questions the participants were asking Henry that he was some sort of leader for this event. He apologized to us for getting sucked into coordinating a few last-minute details for the volunteers, and before excusing himself, he paired us up with a college student, Mike, to guide us on the walk.

The evening was cool, and a bright moon contrasted a few dark clouds rolling in overhead. The clouds were heavy and brought rain down on us as they quickly passed over. We walked a well-marked path through town, and we got to know Mike along the way.

After about an hour of what was a pleasant walk, a car pulled up ahead of us and stopped. Henry got out of the passenger side and joined us.

"My doctor says I'm supposed to walk a little every day, so I saved it for this. Besides, I can take only so much of being a bureaucrat."

We continued the walk at a leisurely pace and for a while Henry spoke mostly with Mike, catching up on his recent doings. I was enjoying listening to them when Henry then asked me what I thought about the event.

"Mike filled me in on *why* we're here, and I think it's very cool!"

Henry nodded.

"Yep, it's a positive thing … you know what surprised me the most about volunteering? When I realized how good it feels to serve others. I know it sounds like crap, but it's true. There's nothing like getting your head out of your navel and looking around at what others need, to make you forget about your problems and make you feel good about your life. You know you're bringing purpose to being alive."

A light rain fell again under another passing bank of clouds and the streetlights shined off the wet pavement in a kaleidoscope of soothing colors. I smelled the rain and earth as we walked and felt nearly intoxicated. Henry finished his thought.

"I concluded long ago there is no point in being on this earth unless we make a positive impact on others and leave the world a better place than we found it. It sounds simple, but I invite you to think deeply on it."

And I did.

My Uncle's words, and conduct with Ruffles, and this hunger walk, were the one-two punch which broke me open, and let the world in.

I came to understand the choices in being human and how we alone decide for ourselves if we will be a positive force in life … or not. Real peace is found in *getting out of our own navel and caring for others.* I never did tell him how powerful this truth turned out to be for me, but I suspect he knew … or maybe not … maybe he was just a farmer, doing what came naturally to him, planting seeds, and moving on.

By the middle of the fourth week of our stay, Jake had the harvest done and Dad hauled the last wagon of grain to the elevators in town. With one day of plowing left to do the next morning. I started when it was just light enough to see my rows. I pushed myself all day and my excitement grew with the end approaching.

On that last workday, Penny brought supper out to me and we talked while I ate. I shared my excitement at being nearly done. She said it would be sad when we left, and I realized she was right. I hadn't thought about it yet. I didn't want to leave.

After finishing the last meal I'd ever eat sitting on a tractor at the edge of the field, and the edge of the day, I felt my worth, something new for me. I relished it for a few minutes, and then pushed on. I was possessed with the need to complete the work. Dusk came and I flipped on the tractor lights. Too soon, I saw the end of the job approaching.

Two rows left ...

My mind, after hours of the rhythmic hum of the tractor working, was satisfyingly blank,

One row left ...

Then it was done.

I motored in from the fields and stopped the tractor just outside the barn, flipped off the lights, and shut it down. Then I just sat there in the silence.

The last bit of dusk held a faint red glow on the horizon, and I listened to a light, cool wind rustling the leaves of the trees where Ruffles lay.

My body was vibrating like a live wire, yet I felt peaceful. Stars started showing themselves and I breathed in deeply, just enjoying the scent of earth and corn and soybeans on the wind, and not thinking of anything.

My mind wandered finally to the notion of how satisfying this work had been and I wondered if all adults felt this good about working. If so, then working might not be as bad as I thought before. My thoughts tapered off again and I was mostly just feeling better than I ever had before.

I started the tractor for the last time and drove into the barn, and parked. I walked to the farmhouse and, in a house filled with people, I didn't find anyone in my pathway to the basement. I fell into bed for a deep and dreamless sleep.

Two days later, we left to go back to California. On our way out to the truck, Henry pulled me to the side.

"You've done well here son, thank you … keep your head out of your navel, and you'll be fine."

And he shook my hand, like I was a man.

The trip home was good, and I began to recognize familiar city names near the end, then, at 10 a.m. on a Saturday, we rolled into my driveway.

Dad and Jake hauled my gear into the house, set it in my room and before I knew it, we stood facing each other in the living room. The end of my adventure had come. Unusual for me, I started the parting conversation.

"A thank you seems kinda' weak, but it's all I got right now. Thanks Dad. Thanks Jake."

Not allowing for any awkward moments, Jake reached to shake my hand, then Dad did the same. They said their goodbyes and I was alone.

Being a teenager, I looked first at the refrigerator, and saw a note.

Paul, in case you get home before expected, there's a sandwich inside for you. Come down to Peggy's house, I'm over there. Love, Mom

I took the sandwich out of the fridge, pressed *play* on the cassette deck, cranked up the volume, and went out to sit on the back patio. The same Credence Clearwater tape which was playing when my adventure began all those weeks ago, was still in the player. *Looking Out My Back Door* spilled from the speakers. As I ate my sandwich, I laughed at the coincidence of the song lyrics.

#

'Just got home from Illinois, lock the front door, oh boy.
Got to sit down, take a rest on the porch.
Imagination sets in, pretty soon I'm singing dute, dute,
dute, looking out my back door ...

#

"Looking out my back door … absolutely friggin' right." I said to no one.

Then, I started thinking about where I'd like to get a job. I was home.

27

Looking back on the whole experience, a lifetime later, we went to harvest the seeds Henry planted the previous spring, but while I was there, he planted more seeds … seeds of a different kind … seeds within me. Seeds to yield crops of self-worth, and of purpose, season after season.

Henry was a hell of a farmer.

So, here I am, 47 years on from *the harvest*, proof of Henry's seeds indeed taking root. I find I want to thank him … and I will when I meet up with him again … and Ruffles … someday … somewhere down the road.

7350 Days

At 1:30 in the afternoon, Erik Hansen was more than an hour early for the first day at his new job. He had to be because sitting at home, waiting to go in had been making him nuts. At 26 years old, he was the newest police officer in the City of Santa Ana, California, and he was finding it hard to contain his excitement.

Technically, he had been an officer for two days already, and he had been to the station on both days processing in. The swearing-in ceremony had been much less formal than imagined, with his oath being un-witnessed by anyone except the uninterested city personnel clerk reciting it to him.

City employee orientation took up the rest of the day and half of the next. The orientation was delivered by the same bland clerk who had sworn him in. Erik spent a tedious first day, and second morning, filling out forms, reading and signing policy notifications, and watching orientation videos.

By the afternoon on the second day Erik was expecting more of the same, but as he arrived back from lunch a Sergeant was waiting for him.

Gus Khiazi was gruff looking, yet friendly in voice, as he greeted Erik and openly sized him up. He shook Erik's hand then told him he was there to show him the ropes and make him administratively self-sufficient. Khiazi took him through the maze of offices and rooms at the station, talking nearly non-stop about how each room was, or was not, useful.

Khiazi also explained everything from processing arrestees, to how to fill out the form requesting replacement duty ammunition, which he would need after qualifying at their firing range each month. After about two hours, Khiazi stopped and was silent. He looked at Erik again in a deliberate way.

"Come with me kid, you've got this. We're going for coffee."

Erik didn't feel like a *kid,* but he didn't let the reference bother him, being sure it was meant in a friendly way. They walked down one flight of stairs and entered a massive underground parking garage. Erik marveled at the dozens of police cars, unmarked units, and surveillance vans.

They passed several officers coming and going in the garage, all greeting Khiazi, who acknowledged them by joking and throwing out casual questions to a few of them. He motioned Erik to the passenger side of a patrol car. Khiazi got in

30

the driver's side and guided the cruiser out of the garage. Khiazi then turned his attention to Erik.

"It's my habit to get with all you recruits for your first cup of free coffee as a real-life copper. I'm stuck in a friggin' office every day now and it's the only time I feel close to the streets anymore."

Khiazi eased the car into traffic and continued talking.

"You know where the term *Copper,* or *Cop,* comes from? It's a word coined in London in the 18th century. Back then police wore wool uniforms with copper buttons, unusual for the time. Criminals used the term as slang for police officers and it spread to general use from there. *Copper* was later shortened to *Cop* as happens with slang over time."

Khiazi continued the impromptu history lesson.

"The slang for police in our time is *Five-O.* You'll hear most of our local punks and criminals use it to describe us. It's from the TV show *Hawaii 5-0.* You know, with Hawaii being the fiftieth state in the union, and they have state police there … Five-0."

They parked in front of a Norm's coffee shop and entered the restaurant casually. Khiazi was in uniform, and Erik was in plain clothes. They moved through the entrance and down the aisle toward a windowed corner booth. It was a novel

31

feeling for Erik as most of the patrons were looking at them intently. Khiazi seemed not to notice and sat facing the entrance. He was relaxed.

"Kid, you're going to learn a million things on this job. One of them is to never, ever, sit with your back to an entrance door. It'll become second nature for you and soon you won't feel comfortable doing it even when off duty."

Khiazi paused, looking to an attractive 40-something waitress approaching them. He smiled at her.

"Two cups, Jackie, and a slice of cherry for me. You want anything? You hungry?"

Erik was too excited to even think about eating and shook his head in the negative. Khiazi laughed softly.

"You rookies are all the same, wound too tight to even breathe. Relax Erik, you've got a 30-year stretch in front of you if you do this right, and it's what we're gonna talk about today … doing it right."

Jackie returned with a pot of coffee and a small plate holding a large slice of cherry pie. She stood very close to Khiazi and was plainly flirting with him as she poured. She asked him in a sultry voice,

"Is there anything else I can get you honey?"

"Yes ... it's like this sweetheart ... you're looking so gorgeous today, I'm about to have a heart attack. When I do, please don't call the paramedics, because I want this vision of you to be the last thing I ever see in this life."

Jackie was beaming.

"Gus! ... my word! that's so lame ... but if true darlin', I just wouldn't be able to bear it. I'd have to give you mouth to mouth and at least try to save you."

They shared a quiet laugh and Erik thought it a fair guess something was going on between them or would be soon. Jackie walked away and Khiazi smiled while watching her go.

"She's a great gal, been flirting with me for five years. She's divorced and I think she's working on being my next ex-wife."

Erik was enjoying Khiazi's sideshow and almost forgot why they were there.

"Sergeant, thanks for showing me around and for bringing me here to talk. I'm sure it's no surprise I'm nervous about tomorrow."

Khiazi nodded.

"I know, I was the same way. Granted, it was different back then, but much is still the same, so I've got advice for you, and I want to answer all the questions that you'll be reluctant to ask anyone else later. This conversation is off the record and you're safe asking me anything today, and I really mean anything.

In my experience recruits ask many of the same questions and I'm here to give you the straight truth about this lifestyle, so let's put you at ease. I'll start with this piece of advice - you must relax in this job, above all else, or you'll never last. You've got 3,750 working days in front of you … pace yourself."

They talked for almost two hours, about what to do, what not to do, and the pitfalls to look out for in his personal and professional life. Jackie interrupted them occasionally, refilling already near-full coffee mugs, and making more advances on Khiazi. Eventually Erik had exhausted his bank of questions and he felt more relaxed about starting the next day.

They returned to the station and prepared to part. Khiazi smiled and shook Erik's hand.

"You'll be fine. You're ready. We've put you on swing shift for training, three to midnight. More action, you're gonna love it."

He paused for a moment, looking at Erik.

"Welcome to the Santa Ana P.D. Officer Hansen."

Erik said thanks and, with reluctance, said goodbye.

The last task of the day for Erik lay ahead. He went to the parking lot and popped the trunk of his car. He took out his meticulously packed squad bag and three uniforms, still in dry-cleaning bags with their new SAPD patches on the shoulders. It was time to move in.

He made his way back to the station's male changing room and went in. Two banks of huge lockers, one on each side of a wide aisle, were the main feature of the room and to the rear were showers, toilets, and sinks. Erik scanned the metal number tags at the top of the lockers and found *his* ... #39.

He double checked everything he was loading into his locker and was now sure he wouldn't be missing anything for his first shift. Erik ended his preparations with pinning his nametag and badge on his uniform shirt and rehanging it. He was ready.

Thinking back on the academy and what he had learned, it occurred to him he was in the best physical condition he would ever be in, and he vowed to stay fit. He left the station appreciating he was living a dream long in the making.

The next day Erik was up early and was going nuts waiting for the afternoon to roll around. Pacing his living room, he tried to watch daytime TV. When he couldn't take it anymore, he left and swung by his folk's house and had some coffee with his mom. This worked for a while, but then Erik just had to go in. He arrived back at the station at 2 p.m. and no one was in the locker room. He took his time getting changed and soon some officers came in and filled the space. The officers entering approached him openly, introducing themselves with handshakes and words of welcome. The last officer to greet him was a tall man, 30 something, with stripes on his sleeves. He came up to Erik like the others.

"Hi, you're Hansen, right? I'm Guillermo Sandoval, but you can call me Guy. Welcome aboard."

Erik took Guy's offered handshake.

"Yes Sir, I'm Erik Hansen. Glad to meet you."

Guy looked around the locker room to the other officers present.

"Did you hear it boys? He called me sir! Unlike you disrespectful losers, he knows an authority figure when he sees one."

One of the other officers responded,

"It's because he doesn't know what a jerk you are yet."

Everyone laughed and Guy, smiling, looked back to Erik.

"Pay them no mind. They'd all be lost without me. Welcome to Santa Ana PD, Officer Hansen. You have coffee with Khiazi yet?"

"Yes sir, yesterday. It was … instructive."

Guy nodded.

"I'll bet it was. You'd do well to listen to what he told you, and please, call me Guy, not sir. Well, you've got more to learn than you can guess, but it's the greatest job on the planet if you have the right approach. My only worry for you is if you'll make probation or not … you've got the most ball-busting, disagreeable training officer imaginable. Frankly, your chances with him are about 50/50."

This caused Erik a stab of worry and he wanted to know more.

"Who is he?"

Guy looked at him with sympathy.

"Yeah, He's a prick, name of Sandoval."

The officers dressing nearby erupted into laughter and Erik felt a sense of relief, understanding Guy was talking about himself.

"You notice the cops all have padlocks on their lockers here? Don't you think it odd? Lockers being locked in a police station of all places?"

Guy didn't wait for a response.

"The reason isn't because things come up missing. It's because you are working with the biggest group of practical jokers you will ever meet, and an unlocked locker is an open invitation."

Guy opened his own locker about a half dozen slots down from Erik's and continued.

"I remember once I forgot to lock mine and I came in the next shift to find a dead and stinking three-foot sand shark hanging inside on a belt hook. These cops around here are all evil. Watch 'em all like a hawk."

In his uniform, feeling both thrilled and awkward, Erik followed the group moving toward the briefing room. Erik was distracted by the sounds of his uniform and gear as he walked. His wool trousers scraping, hi-gloss black shoes squeaking, and his gun belt, with its attachments and pouches, smelling of new leather and gun oil, was crackling.

He was distracted listening to these sounds and almost walked into the doorjamb leading to the briefing room. Guy, who was trailing behind Erik saw and chuckled.

"Easy Grasshopper. The first concept I will teach you is this, don't let your uniform wear you … you are wearing it."

Guy moved slightly ahead of Erik and continued.

"Sit to my left at briefings, and it's a good idea to take notes."

They settled into two of the padded chairs near the middle of a half dozen rows of long tables facing a podium. Erik saw a large map of the city hanging on the wall as a backdrop. He pulled his field notebook from his back pocket, ready to write, and Guy continued the theme of the uniform.

"It's nothing new. All of us feel like a cross between a deep-sea diver and Superman at first. My advice, and this is important, is to forget you are wearing a uniform at all. Behave as if you are just a guy in jeans and sneakers in all your dealings with the public. It'll prevent a false sense of invincibility, but oddly it also will increase your command presence because you won't come off as awkward. Almost everyone will be impressed just by looking at you, but not the ones you want to be impressed, unfortunately."

Guy's gaze was fixed somewhere distant, beyond the windows of the briefing room.

"Killers and monsters will not be impressed with your uniform and it's better for you if your mindset is one of having to deal with them just as a man, not as the symbols of your office."

Erik was struck by the truth of it, and he nodded.

39

A lieutenant walked into the room and stood at the podium. He was dressed immaculately, projecting an air of calmness, confidence, and authority.

"Good afternoon officers. Before roll call I must share with you Officer Elena Lopez came to my office just before briefing and told me she would appreciate it if I didn't inform the group that today is her birthday."

The Lieutenant maintained a deadpan expression.

"I feel badly I didn't know today was her birthday and I must publicly apologize for not being in touch with the lives of my squad like I should be. Elena, I'm sorry, and your secret is safe with me."

Elena flushed, but was smiling as a spontaneous rendition of the birthday song broke out amongst the squad. She stood and gave a graceful but incongruous curtsy in her uniform, daintily holding the hem of an imaginary skirt.

The lieutenant continued,

"Okay, roll call: Atwater, Boyd, Bustamante. …"

And so on, until he got to Erik.

"Hansen … Everyone, if you have not met him yet, we have fresh meat sitting to the left of Sandoval … your military left Ochoa, you're looking at Parker, who's been your partner for seven months."

40

More laughter finally subsided, and the Lieutenant continued.

"Officer Hansen comes to us via the United States Air Force and of late he has been a paramedic for the past five years, prior to completing the Academy last week. Welcome Erik. I am your watch commander, Lieutenant Jensen."

A spontaneous round of applause broke out for Erik and when he stood and curtsied, as Lopez had done a few moments before, he was met with approving clapping and wolf whistles.

The lieutenant went on.

"Hansen, if you are vigilant in not allowing any of these officers to induce you to commit any misdemeanors or felonies, either on or off duty, you and I will get along famously."

Jensen next thumbed through his briefing packet, covering ongoing events and issues in the city. Erik paid as much attention to Guy as he did to the lieutenant, looking from the corner of his eye and writing down whatever the lieutenant was talking about when Guy did. The briefing ended and the officers gathered their gear, chatting among themselves as they headed to the garage. Guy turned to Erik as he popped the trunk on their unit.

"Well, we're not in Kansas anymore. Are you ready?"

41

Erik nodded, stowing his bag. Guy closed the trunk and paused, making eye contact.

"I'll drive for the first week. Then you'll drive. Some key things to remember today, and every day. There are honest-to-God real monsters and killers out there. We will be dealing with them daily, sometimes not even knowing it. The number-one objective on every shift is to make sure you and I both go home, unhurt. We both do whatever it takes to make it happen."

Guy paused, looking thoughtfully ahead after they sat down in their unit and buckled up.

"A key component in this objective is you must know exactly where we are, geographically, at all times. I will drill you on our location until it is automatic, and you can spit out an answer in less than three seconds. You have to be able to call out what hundred block we are on and what our nearest cross street is, effortlessly."

Erik was listening. He could sense how important this would be.

"The next most important thing, Erik, is for you to know where I am and for me to know where you are at all times. There is no such thing as over-communication between partners. Lastly, remember to breathe … and always look for ways to have fun on every call. This is the greatest job in the world and

42

if you're lucky you can milk a 30-year career out of it. Do the math … taking out weekends, vacations, and sick days, we get 7,350 days of frolicking with the public we serve, and this is your first. Let's go have some fun."

And they did.

Guy started peppering Erik to tell him their *20* almost the minute they hit the street. Erik had learned in the Academy, a *20* was jargon for the radio code *10-20*, or *what is your location?* Erik knew the city well, but he was surprised at the difficulty in being able to snap out their location when Guy asked. It didn't take long for a radio call to come in, and they were off to his first domestic disturbance. It was a fight between a drunken wife and a drunker husband. Guy led the husband to a far corner of the living room to talk, while Erik interviewed the wife in the kitchen, still in eyeshot of his partner.

Jesus! Erik thought, *they are both rip-roaring drunk … At four in the afternoon! I wonder how common this is.*

Erik felt like he was doing well until Guy came into the kitchen and briefly looked around. He discreetly picked up a steak knife from the kitchen sink, opened a drawer, set the knife in, and closed the drawer. Guy went back to the living room and deftly maneuvered the conversation with the husband. The husband agreed to pack a bag and leave the house for the night.

43

After the husband left, they talked with the wife for a minute more, then departed, merging their unit back into traffic. Guy recapped a critique of the call, a pattern he would keep throughout Erik's training.

"What are your thoughts on the call, Erik?"

"Well, I know for sure I screwed up when I didn't secure the steak knife."

"You are correct. It's not natural to walk into someone's house and take over, but you must. More of us are killed every year at domestic disturbance calls than are killed at all other calls combined. You must control the scene completely. It's literally a matter of life and death. For practical purposes, you own the house, or bar, or yard, or whatever space you are in on these calls. It is yours to command and control until you leave."

Erik appreciated what Guy was telling him, and more so the way Guy delivered lessons, his style of teaching. Erik knew about himself he wasn't very responsive to emotionally charged corrections. He knew he would be fine with Guy as his trainer because of his calm style of criticism.

They rolled next to a traffic collision, with injuries, and Erik was right at home. He took charge and told Guy to pop flares and guide traffic as he got a first-aid box from the trunk and tended the injured. A paramedic rig showed, and the medics took over the patient care. Guy walked Erik through measuring and photographing the scene, collecting witness statements, and then writing the report.

About an hour later, their investigation was complete. They got back in their unit and Guy pulled into traffic again.

"What are your thoughts on the call, Erik?"

After hearing Erik's recap, Guy agreed Erik performed well and deemed he was properly introduced to accident investigation. Guy knew there were usually traffic units on duty to take over accident investigations, but because of the training opportunities, they would work these investigations themselves for a while.

"A city this large, it sometimes happens we have multiple accidents at the same time and our traffic units are tied up, so we are dispatched to investigate them. It is important to do it right. Lives are impacted and large sums of money surround the facts of accidents. We must truly serve the public and impartially investigate every accident correctly."

Guy continued.

"I see a potential problem, for you in particular though, when it comes to handling injured citizens."

He paused, as if for dramatic effect. It worked. Erik waited for Guy to finish his thought.

"You likely have forgotten more than I will ever know about patient care, and this is good. It's a valuable skill in this job. Just one thing you need to sort out in advance, however. You are no longer a paramedic … you are a police officer."

Guy pulled into a shopping center lot and parked the car in an open area where anyone approaching them from any direction would be easily seen.

"I'll give you an example. Let's say we get a call for a robbery in progress at a bank right now. We roll up just as a robber shoots a bank guard in the chest and jumps into a waiting car, driving away at a high rate of speed. Several citizens see the incident and see you arrive. You are in a one-man car. What do you do? … Hansen! Decide now!"

Erik was stunned by the question. His mind raced and he drew a blank. For the second time today, he felt incompetent and unprepared. Erik croaked out,

"I'd follow the suspect, but I don't know why."

Guy nodded.

"I'll tell you why. It's because you are an enforcer of law and order."

Guy was grinning at him.

"Here's the deal. You will always have to make a judgment call. You can twist this scenario a hundred ways and

46

in one or two of them you might even stop and render aid, letting the monsters and killers get away. You'll have to embrace the idea of what your role is. Is it cold for a trained paramedic to roll right past a man shot in the chest and chase someone he may, or may not catch? Absolutely cold, except for this. Are there citizens present in this scene who can render first aid? Most likely yes. And are there citizens present who are qualified to take down monsters and killers? … most assuredly not. It's a no-brainer son. Do your duty."

Erik saw the logic. Guy continued.

"How would you feel, by the way, if you let a killer get away and he shot someone else, or ran an innocent down with a car while fleeing, or if he killed another bank guard in another robbery a week later?"

Erik understood.

"When faced with split-second decisions like this, try to choose the actions you can perform which others can't. It's hard to go wrong when you're following your training."

Guy started the car.

"A little heavy, I know. Let's go have some fun. We're going to jerk some gang bangers around."

Guy steered toward a residential part of their patrol area, and he talked on the way about the active gangs they dealt with. Guy parked their unit at the edge of a large city park.

"This is a hang-out for the Lime Street Gang, primarily Hispanic with a few whites and blacks in the mix. I know most of the members pretty well and I use them to keep tabs on what's going on."

About a quarter mile distant Erik saw a young teen wearing a baggy white T-shirt and baggier jeans, walking toward them.

"One of my favorites! He goes by *Payaso* for his gang name, meaning *clown* in Spanish."

Payaso saw them and his walk slowed. Guy waved to him to come over to their patrol car before he had too much time to think about running. Guy finished his description for Erik as the gang member approached.

"Payaso and I have a rapport. I took care of his mother a few times when he was younger. Her abusive A-hole of a boyfriend was beating on her a lot, and I put him away on burglary charges. Payaso feels like he owes me for respecting his mother."

Guy mused on this thought for a moment.

"Moms are great leverage with these guys by the way - remember it!"

Guy was parked at the curb on the wrong side of the road and greeted him.

"Qué pasa Payaso?"

The teen nodded and ambled from the sidewalk to Guy's side of the car. Before the car stopped, Erik noticed Guy unholstering his 9mm duty weapon and holding it discretely against his right leg, where Payaso wouldn't see it. Erik did the same and his heart was racing. Were they in some sudden danger? Was this just precautionary? He didn't know.

Payaso ignored Guy's Spanish.

"Officer Guy, what's up homey?"

Guy smiled.

"This is Officer Hansen. He jumped in with us starting today. Erik this is Payaso. He's a heavy hitter with the Lime Street crew."

Erik and Payaso made eye contact and nodded to each other, with neither reaching to shake.

Payaso looked back to Guy,

"So, what's up? I'm chill today. You're not gonna jack me, are you?"

"No, I'm just showing Erik the area and we are also testing out some brand-new secret equipment."

"Secret equipment? Like what?"

Erik was lost before realizing Guy was putting Payaso on in some way. Guy elaborated,

"Yea, we got it installed just today. You know what a polygraph machine is, right?"

"Yeah, like a lie detector, yeah?"

"Exactly! Well, they have a digital generation of these machines now and we are installing them in all our units ... portable polygraphs ... it's the future of law enforcement. We have the first one in the city."

Payaso showed a shadow of doubt.

"Truth Holmes? For real?"

Guy displayed a sincere look and raised his left hand with three of his fingers held up.

"My hand to God. One hundred percent true. Technology has come to the hood, Payaso. The sensors are built right into my spotlight."

Payaso glanced down at the light and Guy used the moment to discretely flip a switch on the siren control box and return his hand to the grip of his gun without Payaso's noticing. Erik understood what Payaso did not. When Guy flipped the switch, all he needed to do for a blast from the siren was use his foot to press a button built into the floorboard. Erik immediately saw the possibilities of Guy's prank.

"In fact, you know what, Homey? My Lieutenant told me to be sure I field test this thing today. You just volunteered!"

"Come on Officer Guy. Don't do me like that. I'm always straight with you!"

Guy looked Payaso over as if deciding something important.

"OK, I'll tell you what. Today really is your lucky day. I have to field test this thing for the lieutenant, but I won't ask you any questions about hard felonies like murder, just drugs and what the gangs are up to, so I won't have to bust you. Deal?"

"Damn Holmes. What are you going to ask me?"

Guy projected his most sincere and fatherly demeanor.

"It's alright. I won't even tell your mom or anyone you were tested? All you have to do is put both hands on my spotlight. Go ahead."

Payaso nervously complied.

51

"Just relax, it's super easy. Tell me the truth now, what is your full name?"

Payaso looked around to insure nobody was listening in and said his full name. Both Payaso and Guy were staring intently at Payaso's hands on the spotlight. Nothing happened.

"Alright, good. Now, tell me a lie. When I ask you what color your eyes are, say they're purple, got it? Purple!"

Payaso nodded and waited.

"Payaso, what color are your eyes?" Guy asked.

"Purple."

At the same moment Payaso replied, Guy pressed the floorboard button with his foot, and a loud, short, wail blasted from the siren on top of the patrol car, causing Payaso to jump.

"Dame Holmes! This is messed up!"

Guy nodded in apparent sympathy.

"Yep, it's Orwellian I'd say - Here we go with the real questions – remember, keep both hands touching the spotlight! What gang are you affiliated with?"

Payaso didn't miss a beat and replied,

"Lime Street Ese, Y Que?!"

Nothing happened and Guy continued,

"Have you, in the past, committed crimes not discovered by the police?"

Payaso bristled,

"Come on Holmes, you said no jail, yeah?"

Guy nodded affirmatively.

"Yes, I promised no jail for you today. Don't worry, I want to keep you out for your mother. She needs you."

Guy asked the question again. Payaso hesitantly answered yes. Nothing happened.

"See there, the truth shall set you free!"

Guy watched Payaso and then asked,

"Do you know the present stash spot for any illegal firearms?"

Payaso looked briefly worried and said,

"No way man."

Just then another loud wail was heard. Guy jumped in with mock surprise.

"Payaso! You were doing good, now you're dogging me?"

Payaso gave his best look of sincerity, pleading,

"Truth Holmes, I don't have illegal guns man, I swear!"

Guy looked at him skeptically.

"Payaso, come clean please. The sooner you come clean, the sooner the polygraph is over. You can't beat the machine."

Payaso caved.

"This is messed up Holmes."

Guy continued,

"Let me ask it another way, I didn't ask if the guns were yours. I just asked if you happened to know the location of any illegal firearms which could injure or kill innocent kids?"

Payaso looked down and nodded. Guy didn't miss a beat.

"See! Don't you feel better about yourself already? Now let's go get those guns off the street. Erik, would you pat Payaso down and assist him to his seat? Payaso, you're not under arrest, but regulations, you know."

Erik was enthralled with the entire exchange and was now having difficulty containing an urge to laugh.

Payaso sat in the back as Guy drove from the curb.

"Where are we headed Payaso? Your place?"

The teen, sullen, made eye contact with Guy in the mirror and rattled off the address.

"You're doing the right thing. You don't want to hold for anybody in a place where it puts your mom in danger, right?"

They arrived at Payaso's house, and he guided them to a dirty wooden footlocker in the detached garage. Erik opened the box and found two semi-automatic handguns and a Mac 9 machine gun, along with about 20 rounds of ammunition in a coffee can.

Erik walked the guns back to their patrol car, securing them in the trunk, while Guy walked back toward the house with Payaso. The teen's mom came out the back door then, looking concerned. She recognized Guy and went straight to him, asking what was wrong. Was her son in trouble?

Guy pre-empted her worry with a friendly greeting.

"Hello Anita. Nothing is wrong. Your son found some guns and he asked us to keep the kids in the neighborhood safe by taking them away."

Both Payaso and his mother looked relieved and Payaso's mom hugged and smothered her baby with kisses and compliments.

Guy used the moment to signal Erik for a quick departure and they were on their way. As they drove off, Erik couldn't contain himself any longer and he howled with laughter. Guy was laughing too, though less strenuously.

"So, what are your thoughts, Erik?"

Erik composed himself and thought.

"Well, I never saw anything like it. We got some guns off the street, and I expect you'll be able to milk the *polygraph* with more results on other bangers for a while. I was wondering if you were going to arrest him or not when we got the guns."

Erik trailed off and another bout of laughter overtook him. Their unit cruised easily through traffic and Guy recapped his own conduct, like he'd been doing with Erik.

"Procedurally, there are several issues with what I did. First, it is highly inadvisable to remain seated in your car when contacting anyone, particularly someone you know to be a bad actor. It will happen from time to time, most often with kids, but don't ever let your guard down."

Guy, his hands on the steering wheel, lifted a second finger as he drove.

"Next, it's not advisable to jerk anyone around while you're on duty. I don't know where the idea came from, but I ran with it. It worked out, but it could still cost me down the road with Payaso and his crew, depending on what he makes of what happened. Your best tools for doing good police work are to be open and honest, contrary to what I did today. You want to build rapport and stay in their business every day. Actionable information almost always comes from them when you are in daily contact."

Guy then changed the subject.

"Erik, what's our 20?"

Erik fumbled the answer and Guy shook his head in mock disappointment.

"All you rookies, hopeless."

Erik sat back, smiling. Police work was much more complex than he had imagined. A few radio calls followed, one a burglary report and the other was a drunken man throwing beer bottles on his neighbor's roof. They stopped another gang member and did a field interview, this time following regular procedure, including getting out of the car, and a *field polygraph* was not administered.

Next, they went to another domestic disturbance call where Erik felt more relaxed than he had on the first, and on each call after, he imagined himself not in a uniform, but in jeans and sneakers. Guy was right; it helped put him at ease.

They took a dinner break at about 7:30 as darkness was setting in. Guy told Erik how the nature of their calls would change after the sun went down; a spike in domestic disturbance calls, more accidents and, a little later, drunk drivers and bar fights could be expected. Their meal finished, Guy stood and removed some bills from his wallet and set them under a saltshaker.

"Put down 15 bucks. These people refuse to let us pay for meals, so we 'tip' what the meal would cost. I'm not sure if they ring it up or let the servers keep it, or split it, but the worst we can be accused of this way is being cheap bastards. Don't ever let the friendliness of citizens lull you into a sense of entitlement."

Erik recognized he was being coached about integrity and he was glad to have Guy as his mentor. Back on patrol, Guy told Erik he wanted to guide him through a few traffic citations. He proceeded to a *hot spot* for violators.

"Sometimes the brass will put pressure on us for a little while to write more citations, and I do have to admit it does change driver behavior in the trouble spots. It's not my favorite thing, but you can rack them up fast when you're looking in the right places. If you're on the prowl for violators, get one of the traffic units on the green channel and ask them where the best fishing is. It helps them out too."

Guy stopped the patrol car along the curb about five car lengths from an intersection controlled by a 4-way stop sign and he left the motor running.

"You watch the first one, then you're on."

As if on cue, a car coasted through the intersection. They could see the driver look their way as he passed. Guy flipped the overhead lights on and accelerated to catch up with the driver, who pulled over. They approached, Erik on the passenger side, and Guy made contact.

"Good evening sir. Would you please turn your motor off?"

The driver complied and Guy continued,

"Do you know why I pulled you over?"

The driver, obviously frustrated, replied,

"Yes, I blew through the stop sign because I'm in a hurry to get home. Damn it!"

The driver fumbled for his license and registration without Guy having to ask for it, and he handed them over to Guy.

"Do you also have proof of insurance, sir?"

Guy waited while the driver produced a card.

"Give me a minute and I'll be back with you."

Guy and Erik retreated to the relative safety of their vehicle, standing behind the open door of the unit on the passenger side and they radioed dispatch with the license and registration info to check for wants and warrants.

The dispatcher came over the radio shortly, reporting this driver clean. Guy finished scratching out the citation and walked back to the driver's window, handing the driver back his documents.

"I'm issuing you a citation for failure to stop at a sign. It's an $80 fine. Your court date and court contact info are on the back. Please sign here. Do you have any questions I can answer, sir?"

"Yeah … I have to ask if you guys have a quota of tickets you have to write?"

Guy casually tucked his ticket book under his arm.

"No sir, we can write as many of these as observed violations dictate. Sir, please believe this is not a punishment. Citations are meant to get a violator's attention and change driving behavior, for the safety of us all."

The driver looked at Guy for a long moment, not knowing if he'd just been insulted or if the officer was serious. He gave up trying to figure it out.

"Can I go now?"

Guy stepped back.

"Yes sir. Drive safely and have a pleasant evening."

The driver pulled away and the officers got back in their unit. Guy scratched some notes on the back of the ticket.

"Always make notes on the back of your citations. You think you will remember the details but trust me, by the time the court date comes around, you won't. Note the weather and road conditions, the driver's demeanor and statements, and if they make any verbal admissions, note them."

Guy swung the vehicle around and stopped the car in the same spot they had previously set up.

"I love this spot. It's like shooting fish in a barrel. What are your thoughts Erik?"

Erik grinned. He liked Guy's consistency.

"It seemed fine. Our officer safety was good. I noticed you had him turn his motor off right away, which seems smart to me. It reduces the chances a driver will change their mind and rabbit, and if they do rabbit, it gives you more reaction time. You were very polite with him given his attitude and I wasn't sure if you were being sarcastic or sincere in answering his question at the end."

Guy nodded.

"All fair observations. Some food for thought; outside of domestics, traffic stops are the number two killer of officers, and don't forget this, more of those deaths and career-ending injuries are from third-party vehicles than from drivers you've pulled over. Always mind your situational awareness and don't get run over on the road."

Erik took this in as Guy continued.

"As for the sarcasm, not really. I cut traffic violators much more slack than I should. When they lash out, usually they are just really upset with themselves and sometimes frightened. Don't forget, you are an intimidating presence to most people, especially when they're the subjects of your attention. For most citizens, a traffic stop is the worst trouble they are ever going to be in. It's human nature. You're gonna make a lot of 'em cry, just by stopping them … they get scared. I'm sure you've already noticed how about 8 out of every 10 drivers tense up in some way when we're behind them."

Erik nodded and Guy went on,

"If they are being jerks, or are drunk, they get what they give, but I've found you don't need a sledgehammer to drive a thumbtack. It's a judgment call sometimes, but the bottom line is, we are here to enforce laws and it's not rocket science. Treat everyone with respect, apply the law as evenly as possible, and if you are cutting slack, do so only when you are 200 percent sure your message has been delivered. There is zero value in making anyone wet their pants, and don't forget karma. Brutalizing people will always come back to haunt you eventually."

They waited less than a minute for another car to run the stop sign. Guy flipped the switch and dropped in behind the speeding car two blocks down. The driver pulled over to the side of the road and Erik felt butterflies in his stomach as he stepped out of the unit. The officers walked up to the car, crossing paths in front of their unit so Erik would be on the driver side. He raced through his officer safety checklist in his mind and took a deep breath to contain his nervousness.

Erik looked for who was in the car and turned for a look behind himself, making sure he was out of the way of traffic. Approaching the driver's window and keeping his gun hand free, he focused on her hands, insuring they were weapon free. The driver, a gorgeous woman in her late 20s, wasted no time in turning on the charm, flustering Erik and amusing Guy to no end.

Erik's nervousness disappeared though as he moved through the citation process and by the time Guy finished critiquing the call afterwards, Erik felt ready for another.

They managed two more stops before a radio call dispatched them to take another burglary report. While they were on the way to the call, the dispatcher came on the radio and changed their call.

"One L 14, cancel and redirect, code three, for a 211 in progress, standby for 20."

Erik knew what *One L 14* meant. *One* designated a unit as a marked patrol unit, *L* meant it was a two-officer unit, and *14* being their specific unit. Erik knew how the dispatch center most often informed units on the nature of a call by using the California Penal Code number. *211* was the penal code for armed robbery. The radio went silent, and Erik's heart was beating wildly. The voice of the woman dispatching the call was calm.

"One L 14 respond code three. A 211 in progress at the Village Liquor store, 2427 Edinger Avenue, cross of Euclid." Erik flipped on their emergency light bar as Guy punched the accelerator.

Erik learned to control his excitement when rolling to an emergency as a paramedic, but this was different ... with overhead lights and sirens blazing they were going to a call where men with guns would possibly be meeting them. Erik thought about it while watching the cross-traffic in upcoming intersections. A beep pulsed through the radio every 10 seconds, alerting all officers a felony call was in progress, and regular radio traffic was on hold.

(Beep) - "One L 14, be advised, One L 8 is backing up, two minutes out."

The officers continued at high speed and were nearing the scene.

"One L 14, the reporting party is across the street from your scene and is reporting two armed suspects exiting now (Beep) - One L 14, suspect one is a white male, mid-twenties, blond hair, white T-shirt, jeans, thin build, with an unknown caliber handgun. Suspect two is a male Hispanic in his mid-twenties, blue baseball hat, black jacket, black pants, medium build, (Beep) with a short shotgun or rifle of unknown caliber."

Guy appeared focused, yet calm.

"Ok Erik, we got this. Breathe slow and deep and let's do this by the numbers."

Erik's pulse was racing some, but he felt in control and unafraid.

The dispatcher's voice returned,

"One L 14, the suspects are leaving the scene in a late-model black Firebird or Camaro, unknown plates, with gray primer patches on the right rear fender. The suspect vehicle is being reported as leaving the parking lot eastbound on Edinger."

Erik knew they were only one long block away and he thought he saw a black car turning onto Edinger in the distance. He pointed.

"I think it's them."

Guy nodded.

"Call it out."

Erik paused for what seemed an eternity, while thinking about what to broadcast, but it was only a few seconds. As their unit neared the now-speeding suspect vehicle he could see it was indeed a black Firebird with primer on the right rear panel.

"It's them."

Erik picked up the radio microphone and, taking a deep breath, he broadcast it.

"Station, One L 14, we have the suspect vehicle in sight and are in pursuit, eastbound Edinger, passing Harmon."

It came to him in a flash, he was now seriously frightened. He wasn't sure for a moment if he really wanted to be a cop or not. He sensed he was close to shutting down mentally, and he fought it. Moments ago, he felt calm and in control, now he felt like he was losing it.

DAMN! ... Not now! Just stay alert and process it later.

And he did.

Erik took another set of deliberate, deep breaths to calm himself. He keyed the mic on the radio.

"Station, One L 14, the suspect vehicle is a black Pontiac Firebird, unknown year, still eastbound on Edinger at 60 miles per hour, now passing Lilac."

Guy grabbed Erik's attention.

"Okay, we're in business now. Unit 8 just dropped in behind us. Remember, whatever it takes, we go home tonight. Soon these pukes are going to bail out and either run or fight. Be ready for both. If they bail, you take the passenger and I'll take the driver."

Erik felt calmed by Guy's demeanor and was grateful for his presence. As they closed in on the Firebird, he saw the silhouettes of the two suspects inside.

"Station, One L 14, the suspect vehicle is eastbound Edinger, approaching Iris."

Erik could see the low-slung Firebird arcing on a right turn. The vehicle hadn't slowed enough to complete the turn and he knew his suspects were about to crash.

"They aren't going to make it."

Erik felt his heart racing and his stomach was queasy. He noticed a heavy metallic taste in his mouth, which he recognized as the taste of adrenalin.

The Firebird was sliding out of control until the driver's side smashed squarely into a telephone pole at the corner. The vehicle portion of the pursuit ended with a sickening and noisy series of crunches, clouds of smoke, and flying debris. Erik saw the robbers being slammed about inside the car and he knew the driver wasn't going anywhere.

Their unit closed in on the scene. Guy cut the siren and stopped their unit about 30 feet from the accident. Erik saw the passenger door open, and the suspect stumbled out of the car, stunned and bleeding from a gash on his forehead.

Erik felt spastic as he tried to get out of the unit and talk on the radio at the same time. As he moved to stand, the cord of the radio's microphone stretched to its maximum length as he held it, and it stopped him from standing fully upright. He took a quick, deep breath and, still hunched over, focused on getting his message out.

"Station, One L 14, suspect vehicle crashed at the intersection of Edinger and Iris. Send fire and medical."

Erik dropped the microphone onto his seat, finished standing, and drew his weapon at the same time. The passenger turned and looked toward him. Erik shouted for him to raise his hands and drop to his knees. The passenger turned and ran. Without any conscious thought, Erik ran after him while holstering his weapon. His sense of danger high, he barely noticed his heart heaving, along with his breathing.

The suspect crossed the front lawn of a house and disappeared down the side yard. Erik pulled his hand-held radio from its pouch on his gun belt. Keying the microphone button with his thumb, he called out.

"Station, One L14, I'm in foot pursuit, heading to the back yard between the third and fourth house on Iris."

Panting as he ran, he continued.

"It's the east side, yellow house on the left, tan house on the right."

Still running, Erik thought his last transmission made him sound like a complete idiot, but he didn't have time to care. He entered the passage and saw a gate at the end, standing open. Erik heard a dog barking and guessed the suspect had gone through there. He followed.

Shaking and feeling nauseated, he came to the back yard of the house where he saw his suspect tumble over a tall chain-link fence which separated the yard he was in from the one behind it. The suspect made eye contact with Erik through

69

the links of the fence and ran. Erik didn't slow at all and within a few seconds he leapt about half-way up the fence and climbed over. While this was happening, Erik could hear other officers talking on the radio and realized he had heard, but not listened to what was said. This was sure to disappoint Guy.

Erik was panting as he again spoke into his radio.

"Station, One L 14, suspect has run through a yard and will emerge on Mayflower, unknown house number."

Thank God for Guy's relentless quizzing on their '*20*' all day, it was becoming automatic. Erik pursued the suspect through a second gate. Looking up, he saw his suspect disappear again around the front corner of the house from the side yard they both were in.

Erik slowed a little, worried if he busted full speed around the same corner, his suspect would have time to set up and could be waiting to shoot him. Erik pulled his gun from his holster, then popped his head around for a look.

There he is! ... running across the street ... Mayflower Street!

"Station, One L 20, Suspect is in the open, northbound on Mayflower ... 800 block."

Erik followed, gun still in hand, and they were both out in the open.

He wasn't sure how long he was chasing this guy; it must have been less than a minute, but it felt like an hour. His body was quivering with exertion and his skin felt like an oily sweat covered him. The suspect was slowing considerably, about fifty feet in front of him, headed for another front yard.

Screw that! I'm taking him down now.

As if brought by angels, another unit rounded the corner ahead of them and headed straight toward the suspect. Erik saw the suspect stop, drop to his knees, and raise his hands above his head. Closing the gap, Erik angled to his left to avoid being in a possible crossfire with the other officer. Erik and the other officer closed in. They were now stationary, about 20 feet from the suspect, with their pistols pointed at him. Erik gulped more air and shouted a series of commands.

"Lay down on your stomach and leave your arms out to the side like an airplane! Do It Now!"

Erik was horrified when his voice cracked in the middle of these commands and half of it sounded, to him, like a little girl shrieking. To his relief, the suspect complied. He half expected him to laugh and get up and start running again.

"Turn your head to the right and face away from me."

Better! No cracked voice this time.

"Don't friggin' move! If you even twitch, I will blow your brains into this pavement!"

The suspect lay still, except for wheezing breaths. Erik looked up at the officer - he couldn't think of his name - and they made eye contact. The officer gave Erik a nod, keeping the barrel of his pistol centered on the suspect. Erik re-holstered his pistol and moved in. His hours and hours of training in the Academy surfaced and he flawlessly grabbed the suspect's left hand, turning and lifting it to a straight-arm lock to maintain control.

"Don't move!"

Erik then made a practiced reach-around to the back of his gun belt, took out a pair of handcuffs, and secured the suspect's hands behind him.

Flooded with relief, Erik felt the chill of the night and took deep pulls of sweet, cool, air. He was too exhausted to move off his suspect just yet, so he stayed still. The covering officer approached, holstering his weapon, and smiled.

Carson! ... Dale Carson is his name.

Carson stepped up.

"Friggin' A, Hansen! You bagged an armed robber on your first shift! Now that's jumping in, brother!"

Erik accepted the compliment with a nod, but he realized he was again blowing procedure by not patting down the suspect for a gun! Erik rolled his suspect onto his side and started searching him for a weapon.

To an observer, it would seem Erik paused only to catch his breath. The truth was he was in a lifting fog. He had forgotten to immediately search for weapons on the suspect.

His shame at the oversight was interrupted when he felt a large metal object in the suspect's waistband. He pulled out what he recognized as a Colt Python .357 revolver. Erik opened the cylinder and saw six cartridges in place. The gun was loaded.

At first, this fact generated no thoughts. His mind was blank. He safely handed the gun to Carson, with the shells removed. Then, without warning, Erik turned to his right and vomited onto the pavement. He stared at the gleaming remnants of Norm's Salisbury steak and peas, spread out on the asphalt, and he felt … better. He tasted the bile in his mouth and didn't mind it, and the fog in his mind was lifting.

Carson laughed, gently lifting him to his feet.

"What? You mean you're not Superman after all? Welcome to Santa Ana P.D, Erik. You'll be fine in a minute."

"Thanks, can you clear dispatch while I advise this gentleman of his rights?"

"Glad to."

Erik talked with his suspect and read him his Miranda rights, while Carson keyed his handheld radio.

"Station, One Mary 8 … One L 14 is code 4, two in custody."

Dispatch acknowledged.

"One Mary 8 copy. All units, copy code 3 traffic is clear."

Erik allowed himself to relax as he accepted that he ran down an armed criminal and hadn't died. His mouth tasted of metal, and he felt dizzy … and elated.

Another unit rolled up and Erik saw Carson flash four fingers as a hand signal to the arriving officers. The sign for *code four, situation stable*. The officers relaxed and, getting out of their unit, walked over.

"Erik just went down the rabbit hole" Carson announced.

"He ran down this armed bandito like a cheetah on a gazelle. He didn't piss on himself either. We might have a keeper here!"

The officers chuckled and Erik managed a grin, then remembered.

"Oh crap! Where's Guy? What happened with the driver?"

Carson was still smiling.

"He's code four. The driver is pinned in the vehicle and fire is still cutting him out. Guy is standing by, talking shit to him."

Only then did Erik notice there were about a dozen residents from the surrounding homes out on their porches and lawns, openly watching them. Carson brought the scene to a close.

"Hector, how about you guys take this gazelle to the station. I'll get Erik back to his papa."

The pair lifted the suspect up then both spoke in unison,

"Nice job Erik!"

"Way to go *officer*!"

Carson gave Erik a head wave to follow him. Carson stowed the suspect's gun in the trunk of his unit and Erik heard spontaneous applause and whistles coming from the cadre of neighbors watching them. Erik eased himself into the passenger seat and was feeling good.

It was a short drive around to the crash scene and Erik thanked Carson for his help as he got out. The traffic on Edinger at the crash scene was still in a snarl, with a lane blocked by emergency equipment. A slow line of cars coasted by the scene; the drivers powerless in their attempts not to look at the activity before them.

Cops, firemen, a car wrapped around a telephone pole, fire trucks, a tow truck, three police cars, all with emergency lights cutting the darkness with red and blue bolts of light – It was a circus, and no one was immune. Erik approached Guy, who was standing behind a cluster of firemen cutting his suspect out of the car. Guy smiled broadly at him.

"Well done young man! I heard you on the radio … and you're voice only cracked like a girl once. Quite impressive."

Erik smiled back.

"I don't know what to think yet. I'm in a daze, I guess."

Guy laughed.

"Don't hurt yourself thinking! We'll run through it later … tomorrow in fact. Just breathe deep for now. This job is all about the breathing."

Guy motioned toward the driver with his chin.

76

"It looks like this scumbag might end up DOA. He's barely hanging on."

Erik looked at him and saw there was a paramedic wedged in next to the driver, holding an I.V. bag and talking with him as some firefighters cut the top of the car off. It occurred to Erik how, just eight months earlier, the paramedic could have been him. He never felt so alive as he did right now.

The rest of their shift was taken up with filling out reports and briefing lieutenant Jensen, who was now on the scene, about what had happened. Jensen told them the incident was making TV news across L.A., and an early news truck had already beamed some good background footage of the firemen and Guy working the accident scene.

"Guy, I think they're going to make a star of you … Erik, you did all the work and won't get a drop of ink out of it. Better for maintaining your secret identity Super Boy. You gentlemen head back to the barn and finish up your reports there. Well done!"

Guy coasted their unit into the station garage, parked and turned the motor off, but didn't move to get out right away. He sat, staring at the wall in front of them for almost a minute, and Erik was content with the quiet. Guy then easily opened his door to exit, and he prodded Erik.

"Come on, let's get you inside before you faint and embarrass us both."

Erik was taken aback, thinking he had been masking his emotional state better. Guy, as if reading his mind, added,

"It's the same for all of us. What is it Khiazi says? 7,350 days?"

They ambled toward the locker room, carrying their squad bags. Guy shot Erik a smile.

"Think of it this way youngster ... now you've got only 7,349 days to go!"

Guy's laugh echoed to all four corners of the parking garage as they reached the doors of the station.

The Headstone

For Les Stanton the past five years had seemed eternally long. He was mentally exhausted and found himself wishing he was more excited about being on this long-overdue vacation with his wife Patty. They were on their third day already, cruising in their Land Rover across Northern Utah. They were listening to XM radio and sharing conversation about their surroundings, but also allowing for comfortable silences between them at times.

Their SUV was packed with luggage and camping gear, and they were without set destinations, other than seeing Dinosaur National Monument and Mesa Verde during their circuit of the Southwest.

For all outward appearances, Les and Patty were a well-off, 40-something couple without a care in the world, and he would have given much for it to be true.

They had stopped at a mini mart in a small town along their route and Les was pumping gas. He looked up to see Patty coming out of the store, bringing with her a large bag of drinks and snacks.

Reseating the gas nozzle, he joined Patty at the rear of the Rover and opened the hatch for her. He helped her by stuffing sodas and bottles of water into their cooler. They worked with the quiet efficiency which only long-familiar pairs can. Finishing, Patty glanced at Les with what he thought of as her *brave face*, and she flashed him a painful smile. Almost natural to her now, Les knew it to be her sadness over the death of their daughter, Olivia.

Olivia died of cancer in the days before Christmas last year, after a heartbreaking five-year struggle for all of them. It was late into the following spring now and their sweet girl was gone forever, with her death still dominating their lives. They both were still grieving for her and doing their best to hide it.

Les felt helpless when he thought of his loss of connection with Patty. There wasn't any anger, or bitterness, or blame between them. They both understood the other was not responsible for what happened, yet their sadness was so profound it crippled them both.

Neither could reach out and soothe the other just yet. They spent long hours searching for ways to give comfort to each other and get on with a connected, happy life, but so far it eluded them. Without talking about it much, they both hoped this journey would bring some peace and some connection back to them.

We'll see, Les thought as he smiled at Patty and closed the hatch.

I don't know what else to do, but I have got to get my head out of my ass, get busy living my life, and taking care of her.

With that resolved in his mind, they were back on the road. Shortly though, Les became aware his thoughts had rambled from the scenery and his resolve to be happy again, to thoughts about death. He didn't have a thought about death which didn't lead him into lengthy, and pointless, reflections on the meaning of it all. He was sick of it.

Following a secondary southbound highway, along the western slope of the Rocky Mountains they camped or checked into a motel in the afternoon each day, wherever they found themselves, and kept their pace purposely slow.

They dipped into Northwestern Colorado and the nature surrounding them was astonishing in its springtime beauty.

Morning sunshine and chill air washed over them. Winding their way through the mountain passes with their windows down and the heater going full blast, they were comfortable, and it was awesome to them. They could smell pinesap, wet grasses, and the high alpine air - there was nothing like it.

They saw groves of quaking aspens, with young Spring leaves rattling, nestled at the foot of still snowcapped mountain peaks, looking close enough to touch. Along the lower shoulders of the peaks, meadows blanketed the slopes and were cut with endless streams and rivulets, all lined with patches of bright columbine flowers.

Columbine ... wasn't that where those two high-school kids shot up their classmates and teachers a few years back? Right here in Colorado, wasting a dozen lives or more?

There it was - death nagging at him again. He hardly noticed anymore when his thoughts were straying there. He forced himself to stop thinking about Columbine, knowing it would be replaced by something similar soon enough. More than anything, he wished he could break his obsession with death.

Les and Patty journeyed on and shortly they were stopped on the roadway. A large herd of cattle was crossing their path, headed for a fresh meadow on the other side of the road. Les had never seen such a thing and thought it interesting. Tending to the herd were five horse-mounted cowboys, each looking as if they'd been picked by central casting for a John Wayne movie.

Les and Patty listened as the rider's half circled and prodded the herd with a delightful rhythmic series of words, whistles, and flicking snaps of their leather reins. The movement of cattle and riders was efficient and relaxed. Les looked over to Patty, feeling her gaze, and saw she was smiling the first real smile he'd seen from her in months. She spoke.

"Isn't this fantastic? I've never seen real cowboys before. They look so real!"

They both laughed.

"I'm such a tourist!" she continued. "But look at him there!"

She was pointing out the rider nearest them, young, with a weathered face, handsome, and confident in the saddle.

"I swear he's the Marlboro Man."

Les agreed, looking at the passing rider, who gave them a cool, but friendly tip of his hat. They responded with smiles, Patty adding a subdued hand wave. Les thought about the irony of the Marlboro Man in the ad campaign, dying, as Les had heard it, a horrible death of lung cancer.

Enough! he screamed inside himself ... *I've got to stop this!*

To break his own spell, he turned to Patty.

"This is a fun trip so far, don't you think? Are you getting hungry yet? "

Patty was. With the cattle safely across the highway, they motored on with an eye toward somewhere to stop and eat.

A few miles up, as if to fit their need, the road guided them into a shallow valley holding a small resort. They saw an appealing roadside restaurant there, perched at the edge of the river which had been following their roadway off and on for the past few hours.

Pulling into the graveled lot, they parked in front of the restaurant and went inside. They saw through the back windows there was an enormously large deck. They asked the young hostess if they could sit out there, and they were guided to their table. The deck was set with flowers spilling from half-barrel oak planters and the sturdy picnic tables were all covered with red and white checked cloths. Atop each table was a cardboard six-pack beer box, holding condiments and napkins, and the deck was edged with a thick split-wood rail.

Adding to the tranquil space were a half-dozen hummingbird feeders, hanging about the edges of the deck on tree limbs, framing an amazing view of the river sliding past. The space was finished off with discreet outdoor heaters and hidden speakers. They settled in at their table and heard the tune *Pocahontas* by Neil Young softly flooding the deck. Not surprisingly, some dozen or more beautiful hummingbirds had taken note of the feeders and were busy darting in and around the deck's edge.

Les and Patty took some joy in watching the birds fussing with each other, just feet away from them. Les was feeling almost happy as they talked, sipping their iced teas, and eating.

How long has it been since I've felt this good?

He couldn't remember for sure. Lunch finished, Les didn't want to leave. He stalled their departure by reaching into his knapsack and pulling out the map he was using to guide their journey. Looking at Patty, he felt there was still a lot of love between them, even though they were estranged by grief.

This distance between us is over! I've got to reach her again, and it starts now!

Les waited until Patty finally met his gaze.

"Do you want to see if we can find an old mining town, a ghost town?" This area is supposed to be riddled with them."

Patty lit up at the idea.

"Yea, it might be really fun! Can you see any on there?"

Les, looking over the map, wasn't sure.

85

"Well not exactly, but it shows all the unpaved roads and this one here takes us to the cut-off highway we need if we want to keep heading south. It'll take longer, but it will get us there, and who knows what we'll see."

Patty looked to where he was pointing on the map and asked,

"Is it drivable all the way through, do you think? I'd worry about getting stuck out there."

Les considered it.

"I doubt it would be on the map if it's not drivable, but we have a four-wheel drive and the worst that could happen this time of year is, we'd have to turn around and come back."

Patty was enthused.

"Let's do it then!"

They drove on for about an hour and found the turn-off they wanted. The dirt road was surprisingly smooth and Les guessed it was kept maintained for logging operations. Driving much slower off-road, their windows were all the way down, and they rolled on, into the forest. Miles ticked by and they noticed more wildlife, and creeks with dozens of *cute waterfalls*, as called out by Patty. Over the next two hours they saw no sign of civilization but the road itself.

Les was just beginning to worry a bit about being lost when they rounded a gentle curve and saw what they'd been seeking, a ghost town. Up a gentle slope, the *town* consisted of a few abandoned buildings - a general store, a barn, a schoolhouse, or church (or both in one?), and several houses and smaller shops were scattered about. The scene was made vivid with the buildings presenting weathered wood, and the little of what remained of their flaking, washed-out, paint.

Les parked along the roadside at the crumbling general store and they got out to explore. To the left of the town site, on its own low hill, they saw a graveyard bordered with an old, ornate wrought iron fence. The fence was waist-high, with more rust than metal holding it together. There were no signs of any recent presence, and the site was strangely quiet.

They turned their attention to the buildings, all of which looked to be failing. They cautiously walked through them, finding nothing of interest after so many decades, but still feeling the age and history of the place, nonetheless. The buildings, with doors and window glass long gone, had a faint odor of mold being their main feature.

After about 15 minutes, they'd seen all the town itself and they drifted to the adjacent low hill where the town cemetery was. Patty took his hand instinctively, giving him a gentle squeeze as they walked … something she hadn't done for months. Les, feeling her warmth, squeezed in return.

After the short walk to the gate, they paused at the entrance. They could see the most substantial remnant of the fence was the archway, forged with an arbor of hundreds of small, well-crafted iron ivy leaves, creating an oddly welcoming entrance, which invited them in. The left-side gate was still connected to a rusted support post and was hanging crookedly open, while the right-side gate was long missing.

Les and Patty entered, gradually wandering apart, while quietly strolling past grave markers and taking in the stillness of the place.

Perhaps 200 headstones in all were spread out in even rows across, in what Les estimated to be a space of about five acres. The headstones looked almost stark against a uniformly low and mossy ground cover, but when examined up close, even the headstones were softened by decades of harsh mountain weather.

The stones were of many sizes and shapes, in various states of repair. Some were intricately carved while others were plain. Some of the headstones were beaten down by time, with their granite lettering so weathered as to be unreadable, and these stood next to headstones just as old, but in great condition with still sharply etched messages to the living, a mystery Les could not explain.

He'd never walked through a cemetery out of curiosity before, let alone an abandoned one, and he became fascinated.

Who were all these people? What led them to live and die here of all places?

As he walked by the markers, reading them, he wondered about their lives. From the dates on most of the headstones, Les guessed that people had been buried here from the early 1850s until about 1919.

This must have been a mining town. It just dried up and blew away when the ore ran dry.

The most recent headstone he saw was one for a World War I soldier:

Edgar Van Zandt
Born: March 2nd, 1899
Beloved Husband and Father to a son he has not yet met.
Killed in the Battle of the Ardennes, Belgium
April 12th, 1919

How did they get him home? Almost all the soldiers killed over there were buried there - or is this just a marker?

There was a tattered, hand-sized American flag staked at the base of the headstone.

How odd! Who would mark this old grave? This flag must be less than a year old and someone still cares enough for this old soldier to come out here to remember him.

Taking a slow, deep breath, Les looked up and watched Patty reading a marker two aisles over. At that moment he saw her body run a shiver. He was certain she was beginning to feel as spooked as he was.

Walking the last row of markers, he felt charged with an unexplained feeling, as if he was in a mysterious place and his own body quivered with excitement.

What is this feeling?

He couldn't recall a time when his senses were so tuned, his awareness so focused. Sight, sound, smell, touch, all peaking. It was the strangest mixture of elation and dread he'd ever known.

To stem his building unease, he turned his thoughts from himself, outward. He saw the sun beginning its long, slow slide toward the west, and rays of light cut at shallow angles through the stands of bordering trees. The air was warm but balanced by a perfect breeze. What seemed a silence to him when they arrived, he now heard as a quiet symphony. Birdcalls, insects buzzing, a distant brook babbling over smooth stones, breeze-stretched branches creaking, all of these were led by the clattering leaves of thousands of aspens.

It made for an intoxicating background and Les, without deciding to do it, let go of his internal dialogue and let himself soak into the scene.

He became aware of himself again gradually and moved on down the aisle. Patty rounded the last row of graves and was strolling toward him, still reading markers as she passed. They met near the middle of the row and before them was the most curious headstone yet.

It was lower, but thicker, than most of the others. The slab was a dark-gray granite, with a lighter gray lettering, finely chiseled. The stone was tipped slightly backward and was richly carved with script and design. Curiously, by this time there was only one shaft of afternoon sunlight breaking through the trees, making its way to the cemetery floor. The shaft of light was encircling just the stone they stood in front of, as if a spotlight was shining on it.

Les reached for Patty's hand. He held it, looking around the cemetery. Then he looked at her.

"Darlin', I don't know about you, but this day, this place, the sun circling this headstone, the quiet, the sounds ... this place is ..."

He couldn't find words to finish his thought, but he didn't need to. Patty finished his thought for him.

"It's magic! I feel we are supposed to be here."

Their eyes locked in understanding and he felt relief that she understood. They turned their attention back to the headstone. Most notable was a set of carved angels in profile, facing each other from opposite edges of the stone. Their arched wings conformed to the curve of the weathered granite.

The angels bowed toward each other, hands clasped in prayer, with their foreheads meeting at the top of the dome. They were made fierce by the weathering on their granite faces and they looked to the etched words in the center of the headstone.

The soul being guarded by these heavenly protectors was a young woman.

Olivia McKay
Born August 12th, 1850
She died a Fever - age 23 in the year of our Lord 1873
Sweetness and goodness sprang from her in life.

Les gasped in surprise at the same moment he heard Patty doing the same.

"What the ...!"

A shiver of animal shock bolted through him, head to toe, and it took him more than a moment to reason, then accept, that the name of his daughter here was just a coincidence.

Les and Patty looked up at each other briefly, then back at the headstone. Les sighed.

Another one, so young ... just like our Olivia ... one who today would have survived a fever for a fuller life than the one she was given.

Unlike many of the other headstones they'd seen this day, there was additional script etched below her name and dates ... an epitaph. It was a line of verse, Olivia McKay's final message in eternity to any among the living who would ever pass her way.

As you are now, I once was, alive and free
As I am now, soon you will be
Prepare yourself to follow me

The message stunned them in its simplicity and rawness. Les reacted by jerking upright and taking a step back from the stone. Patty seemed to have the same reaction, and they looked at each other with a mix of fear and interest. Without a word, they turned together and headed back to their vehicle.

A quick walk through the cemetery gate became a near sprint by the time they reached the Rover. They burst out with nervous laughter as they climbed in and sped up the road away from the *town*.

Safely away, they were laughing not at what they'd read, but the reaction of their bodies to what they'd experienced and their lack of control in running away from it.

Rolling on just a quarter mile further, Les saw the dirt road change to pavement. He realized this ghost town sat close to the highway they'd been looking for at the end of the logging road on their map.

He stopped at the intersection to the highway, trembling. He felt back in control of himself, but they were both still breathing with a little excitement and, seeing Patty was as affected, knew neither of them wanted to say anything just then.

Les then made the connection. What was affecting him today, and indeed in all the months since his baby Olivia's death, was his deep dread of death for himself.

Something had happened today … death's grip on his thoughts and dreams, he knew, was now broken. Les embraced the idea that they were living in a world of mystery and love, and he had just turned a mental corner. His mind could settle into a place where thoughts of death may be a companion, but those thoughts would no longer rule his life.

At the intersection in front of them was a road sign and he saw it as a metaphor for the understanding he just gained - Leadville to the left, Durango to the right.

Whether he chose to go to Leadville or Durango, death waited for him, at the end of either road - but what of it? His only choice in the face of death was as it always would be … to accept it, and enjoy the drive, whichever road he chose. It was a true epiphany.

All he could do, all anyone can do when wrestling with the certainty of their mortality, was to fill their hearts with as much love and joy as they could find along the way. It was enough for him … he could live with it.

His spirit felt lighter than any time he could remember since his girl was sick and his obsession was falling away from his heart like a weight, right there, sitting at the crossroad.

Considering the road ahead, Les took a deep, calming, breath. He looked at Patty, who met his gaze, and smiled his first real smile in months.

Looking down both roads at the intersection … he chose one. With controlled abandon, he eased the Rover onto the highway, and they were gone.

Like their recent teacher, Olivia, they were down the road of time.

Thicker Than Water

Two brothers grew up in the sheltered and sunny climes of southern California, in an age before cell phones, Play-Stations, or digital HDTV. They launched themselves from their bikes off wooden ramps and listened to top 40 hits on transistor A.M. radios, all in a time when skateboards still rolled on metal wheels and laundry was hung out to dry on clotheslines in the backyard. As far as the brothers were concerned, they were on the cutting edge of heaven and life was a grand adventure.

The boys, a year and a half apart in age, shared friends, clothes, meals, pets, and black and white TV shows at night. More than this, they shared the Pacific Ocean. They enjoyed near-daily adventures around their hometown of Redondo Beach which was, in those days, a quiet, thinly populated, middle-class town. They couldn't have known it then, but the bonds they forged would serve them well later in life.

As is typical of brothers, Alan, the oldest, oversaw their doings, and Steven, the youngest, was in dutiful agreement with this arrangement. Their father was an engineer, working for one of the many south-coast aerospace companies fueling the Cold War at the time, and their mother was among that last generation of stay-at-home moms. Their nuclear family wasn't complete, however, until Mom relented and allowed into their home, a lovable brown puppy, who the boys, not-so-creatively, named *Brownie*.

Surrounded by an amazing assortment of cousins, aunts, uncles, grandparents, friends, and adopted neighborhood parents, they never felt isolated. Their world was one of freedom, but with the security provided by nurturing adults who guided them. They were led to organized sports and outdoor activities, all with hardly any leash on them. Life never would get any better and the boys sensed it.

While sprouting in this environment, the relationship between the brothers was forged with a bond of squabbling familiarity. Alan sometimes would pick on his younger brother, but only God could help any poor bastard who ever messed with Steven ... and so it goes with brothers.

Being of an age where neither of them thought about these things, though, they both were content with having been issued to each other and they shared, more than anything, a sense of adventure. For them, this was what life was about. Everything was looked at in terms of having fun and uncovering mysteries.

And so they did, spending their summers and weekends body surfing at the beach, exploring groves of eucalyptus trees and ponds, and jumping off the city fishing pier to dive for quarters thrown to them by tourists. Other favored adventures were riding bikes with their friends from dawn 'til dusk, scrounging pop bottles for enough money to buy water balloons, or better yet, to buy a ticket for a triple feature at the old Fox Theater.

The Fox was a run-down, art deco, movie palace, built in the 1920s, sitting right next to King Harbor … price of admission … 50 cents!

This then was how they grew. They were loved, and confident, and no one loved them more than their mother.

Mom was subtly, but deeply involved in their lives. She sat with them for homework, she was their Cub Scout den mother, and was active in their school PTA. She moved the boys into endless other activities, with swimming lessons, YMCA basketball, flag football, Little League, and junior lifeguards being but a few. There was never a birthday or any kind of holiday which didn't get celebrated in some over-the-top fashion, including decorations, friends, and family on hand, and lots of warm attention.

Mom was happy all the time, and the boys would often find her singing like an angel to herself around the house. It wasn't any wonder to them that all the neighborhood kids liked hanging around their house while they were plotting their next adventure. Awesome snacks and her warm acceptance for all of them was the norm.

The boy's father worked a lot, but he was very present with them when he was home, especially on weekends. He was approachable, unlike some dads, and he was a great storyteller. While Dad was feared when they misbehaved, he was nurturing and never missed an opportunity to teach them things. He taught them everything from the proper use of Q-Tips to clean their ears, to building sturdy wooden ramps to launch their bikes from. The boys, for their part, always enjoyed these teachings.

Like most 11-year-olds, Alan hadn't spent much time contemplating how fortunate he was, but the fact forced itself upon him one weekend when he gained a deep appreciation for his brother. It began with Dad coming home from work early one Friday, which he always did when they were going camping. The boys arrived home from school together and their excitement grew when they saw him emerging from the garage and loading their bulky 6-man canvas tent into the family VW Bus.

Their folks liked getting to the campground on Friday evenings because it gave them an extra night out of the house and allowed for their entire Saturday to be enjoyed without driving. The boys, seeing what was afoot, ran to their rooms, threw down their book bags, and joined in the packing of the VW. Mom and Dad had already stowed their large, green, Coleman cooler, and a few boxes of food before the boys got home. This left them to pack their own clothes and sleeping bags.

Camping prep was routine for them, but they were still filled with excitement. Finally ready, they all piled into the VW, with Brownie bounding in first, for their journey to *the lake*.

Dad, before becoming an engineering techno-warrior, fighting Russians to the death, was a Boy Scout. He relished teaching his boys outdoors skills – making campfires, knife sharpening, knot tying, fishing, and hunting. There seemed to be no end to what he knew. The boys ate it up.

As for Mom, she enjoyed fussing over them on these trips and she loved the togetherness of the campsite. Most of all, though, she loved making s'mores, which she insisted on making every evening around the campfire.

On this trip, Dad sat the boys down by the campfire after dinner on the first night. It was still a little bit light out and too early for s'mores, so he chose this time to produce a three-pronged spearhead from his gear bag. The trident was smaller than his hand, but with wicked-looking barbs at the end of each of the three prongs. Both boys' eyes widened while watching him handle the spearhead, turning it slowly and moving it from one hand to the other while he talked.

The tines of the spear glistened in the firelight and Dad explained it was for spearing fish and for gigging frogs along the banks of streams and lakes.

Dad always went into teacher mode when introducing anything new to them and they understood this was the price of learning anything fun. They contained their excitement as best they could and listened, learning a few things in the process. He explained the safe use of the spear, consequences of misuse, and techniques for stalking their prey.

He ended their talk with an assignment. He told them to go into the woods, with their last bit of daylight, to find the longest and straightest tree branch they could for the spear shaft.

The boys eagerly responded and with Brownie barking and running ahead of them, they were off and into the woods. Alan and Steven searched randomly for the perfect branch. After rejecting dozens of candidates, Steven found a goodish branch of birchwood, straight, about five feet long, with just a few small knots to be smoothed down.

Alan looked over the branch in detail and, deeming it worthy, he gave grudging praise to Steven for the find. They scrambled back to camp, guided by their campfire in the gathering dusk.

They joined their dad at the fire ring and waited while he examined their find. Dad looked it over with the same seriousness as Alan had and he pronounced it a fine shaft. The boys were relieved.

The rest of the evening was spent sitting around the fire, in their well-worn lawn chairs, making s'mores, telling ghost stories, and listening to their folks tell them stories about their childhoods. As they listened, each brother took turns whittling knots and bark from the spear shaft, honing it to a straight, smooth perfection.

Dad then showed them the *tricky part* of tapering the end of the shaft for seating the spearhead, making it not too thin, not too thick, but just big enough to grip the sleeve of the spear. He explained this was the most critical part of the process because it did no good to spear an animal, only to have it injured and escaping if the spearhead slipped off its shaft.

When the spear was finished, the boys took turns holding it and making practice jabs into imaginary bears and wolves, getting a feel for its balance and weight. Too soon, their folks secured their camp for the night, and hung their Coleman lantern inside the tent.

Alan and Steven both were dreading the idea of the entire night of sleep standing between them and taking the spear to their prey. Eventually, however, they did sleep, and they dreamt the dreams of hunters.

Morning came and they woke to the sounds of Mom cooking just outside the tent, and the smell of eggs, pancakes, and frying bacon pulled them the rest of the way to wakefulness. They dressed, raced through their morning grooming routines, and sat to eat. They were struggling by this time to balance their attention between breakfast, and the spear.

Dad, up and dressed already, was sitting by the morning fire, sipping coffee from a blue enamel mug. He was smiling while watching the boys eat and making light conversation with them.

With breakfast done, Dad told the boys he needed to stay to do things around camp. He let this news set in for a moment and explained.

"Boys, I'd love to go with you today, but I have to stay here and help out with firewood and such … you're old enough to manage without me."

Alan noticed Mom smiling at Dad, and wondered why, but the thought was pushed away by his excitement to get going. Dad quizzed them on what supplies they were bringing, and what to do if they got lost. He recapped safe spear-handling practices while checking their gear and examining their napsacks.

The boys were both feeling grown up as Dad ran through their check-out. They wore a kid-sized, military-style web belt with a canteen and a leather-sheathed hunting knife, slung from their belts *just so.* They finished their pack adjustments while Dad gave them final instructions.

"Be back before dark, be safe, look after one another, and have fun."

That was it … they were free to go. Alan grabbed up the spear and Steven called for Brownie. The trio were off toward the lake, and they were ready for all the unknown dangers which were surely ahead.

The spear was the central preoccupation of the day. They were starting too late to find frogs, so they decided to build a raft to fish in deeper water than the shore. They spent a couple of hours on this project and used the light rope each of them carried in their napsacks to fashion a well-done craft. During the build, Alan came to admire a few things about Steven.

Alan hadn't noticed before, but Steven was very good with rope and knots. Steven also put forth a few great ideas about log placement and lashing points, thus making their raft even more seaworthy. For his part, Steven looked up to his big brother, earned or not, and Alan realized for the first time in his young life maybe the world didn't revolve around him, and he should be grateful for having such a cool brother, and dog, and parents, and … and … everything.

Alan dealt with this epiphany by ordering Steven back into the woods with him to find two long rafting poles to push them around the lake. They launched their raft, and the next few hours were unremarkable, except that they were perfect.

After floating for a long while, they beached the raft next to a small stream emptying itself into the lake. Following the stream, the boys hiked up about a half mile with the objective of damming it at some spot to make a *swimming pool*. They soon found a natural pool, about two feet deep. They toiled for a time and filled the downstream side of the pool with stones and branches.

Some of the water still made it through their dam, but despite the run-off, within minutes the size of their pool about tripled. They both were able to fit in the pool and they soaked themselves, letting the cold water flow over them. The sun cut through the trees, keeping them warm, while the stream kept them cool, a balance which can only be noticed and appreciated by kids.

They followed their swim with a lunch of peanut butter and jelly sandwiches and potato chips. Content and full, in the afternoon shade, the boys took a rare, but short, nap. Upon waking, they were rested and eager to continue their hunt.

While hiking back downstream to the lake they amused themselves by searching the streambeds along the way, looking for gold, crystals, or evidence of alien spacecraft, none of which were found, but all of which were known by the boys to exist.

Once back on the lake, they tried their hand at spear fishing from the raft again but were unsuccessful in sticking any of the few fish they saw. Undeterred, they beached the raft (dubbed the S.S. Fort Knox by now) and deliberated on what to do next.

Being the explorers that they were, they knew if they walked around the entire lake, they were bound to find their camp, but were not quite sure how long it would take, and if they could be back by dark. Alan, ordinarily decisive, was having trouble with what they should do. Steven told him he would go along with whatever Alan decided.

"Like Dad always says, blood is thicker than water ... I go where you go."

Alan felt humbled and he was resolved to earn Steven's trust. Emboldened, Alan decided to go for it and, with the type of courage reserved for the innocent, they were off to circumnavigate the lake. The trail following the edge of the lake was about another five miles long, but this was unknown to them.

They felt as they imagined Columbus must have when looking for landfall. The entire day so far, they'd not seen another living soul, but for each other. This was about as close to loneliness as the boys knew.

Alan didn't know if Steven thought about this, but he did, and in a wave of generosity he handed the spear to Steven.

"Here, you carry it for a while. My arm is getting tired."

Steven grinned from ear to ear, taking the lead on the trail, behind Brownie of course, and the afternoon wore on. The boys trudged ahead in silence, looking at the dragonflies and butterflies dancing around them and hearing the occasional blue jay mocking them. They saw squirrels and chipmunks in abundance, but Dad prohibited them as prey.

"You never kill an animal you don't plan on using for food, ever ... do you understand? It's fish and frogs for you two today."

Alan watched as the sunlight dimmed a little and he still didn't know how far they were from camp. This worried him, but he kept going without saying anything about it. Steven, if worried, did not show it, setting the pace for a fast hike. Another 20 minutes farther on, they stopped for a rest and drank from their canteens.

While sitting, they heard it ... up ahead, about 20 or 30 yards ... frogs croaking at the lake's edge. Giving each other a silent nod, they tightened up their gear and Steven lifted the spear to Alan. Alan looked at Steven, then nodded for him to take the lead with the spear.

They found the source of the croaking and Steven crept up within about four feet of a big bullfrog. Taking careful aim, he gigged the frog, which went silent. Walking back a few steps, Steven held up his prize to show his brother. Alan smiled and pulled the frog off the spear with a single jerk. Both understood they needed to contain their excitement and be silent until the hunt was over. Alan motioned Steven back for another try.

Steven went in and soon came back with another fat frog. Alan pulled it off the spear, placing it on the grass next to the other one, and took the spear for his turn. They worked a little longer to bag two more of the by now spooked army of frogs. The boys were practically dancing with excitement, comparing their kills, and complimenting each other's hunting skills.

Alan then looked at the sun nearing the horizon. Not betraying any concern, he said they should pack their catch and get moving. Brownie again took the lead, sniffing the trail here and there as she trotted before them, guiding them up the trail. After about half an hour more, dusk was settling in and Alan was officially nervous about the approaching darkness, but he could not - and would not - show it to Steven.

They continued for another 15 minutes until, at last, they saw a campfire at the edge of the lake, about another half mile ahead. Their trail was still visible, but it wouldn't be for long. They jogged and just as twilight was setting in, they burst into camp.

Mom was starting dinner and greeted them casually as she moved between their Coleman stove and the campfire grate, cooking fried potatoes and burgers. She said she wasn't sure there was enough to eat, and she sure hoped they brought something back to go with hamburgers. The boys produced the frogs and Mom, and Dad pronounced the meal saved. Dad showed them the butchering process for frog legs, then he set up a cast iron skillet on the campfire grate.

Melting a little butter into the pan first, he then laid the frog legs into the pan, and sprinkled them with a little salt before he sautéed them. Once done, Dad forked the legs onto a paper plate and ate one first.

"Humm, that's good boys … tastes like chicken!"

They laughed and were encouraged to try them, eating two of the legs each while standing around the campfire. Watching Mom eating her frog legs made them laugh. She played off loving their taste, when her grimacing made it clear she didn't care for it at all. They moved to their picnic bench and through the rest of dinner the boys took turns recounting their adventures for their folks.

For Alan, this day was as close to a perfect as he would ever know. None of the four of them knew it, on this perfect night, in their warm family circle, their lives would be changed forever in less than half a year. Others may have seen signs of their parents' marriage being at risk even earlier, but for the boys, it was not a thing which would ever occur to them.

Their life in Camelot came to a crashing end in one single night, the following spring.

Their folks sat them down in their living room one evening, in a formal and uncharacteristic way. Their dad told them they (their mother and father) decided they were not going to be married anymore. Dad tried to explain.

"It doesn't mean we don't love you boys anymore; it's just sometimes adults grow apart."

The boys were devastated and cried openly … and their mom cried in silence with them. Dad didn't cry and this bothered Alan a lot. He couldn't look at his dad during the whole time they talked. He felt like Dad was divorcing all of them. Without saying so, Alan blamed himself for whatever he'd done, or whatever defect of his, was causing Dad to leave them all like this.

In truth, Alan wasn't mature enough to understand what was happening and he was just an 11-year-old mess. Alan shut down and refused to ask any questions when invited to do so.

Steven asked of his father just one question,

"When will we see you?"

Dad said they would see him every other weekend and they could call him anytime they wanted, and he'd still see them at their team games and activities. Steven accepted this in silence. Alan was sure it was a lie, and he did not accept it ... also in silence.

Steven, for his part, was hurt to a depth he could never hope to explain. He didn't blame himself, and he couldn't blame his father or his mother ... he didn't know how, and all he could do was feel loss and a sadness which wouldn't be equaled again in his life.

Dad left the same night, taking with him a bag of belongings. As he left, he changed their home to a house, with a single, deafening *click* of the front door latch dropping into place behind him. For decades afterward Alan never called where he lived his *home*. It was a word he never did get comfortable with again, even as an adult.

Mom and the boys struggled to understand and to be happy after Dad moved out, and they looked to each other to fill the gaping hole in their lives. In time, it began to work. They talked more and helped each other more. The boys saw and believed their mom would die before ever leaving them, and this stopped their slide into fear.

Mom wasn't happy like she used to be, but she was strong and determined and this gave the boys some confidence. They did what they could see needed doing and whatever she asked of them, which wasn't much. They grew closer over time and Dad's presence in their thoughts and lives was fading.

Mom took the best paying job she could find, on the graveyard shift as an operations manager at some company the boys had never heard of, but even with this, their standard of living deteriorated significantly. They were poor. The boys could see Mom's constant worry and they felt powerless to fix it.

Watching her fatigue and sadness over weeks and months they understood Mom most needed them strong. Inside themselves, though, they were both still sad and angry.

The boys grew and time moved on. After a few years the boys spent less time together and were growing apart some, but their bond with each other, and their mom, held tight, at a deep level, while their dad became an occasional bothersome stranger in their lives. Dad asked Alan once, on one of his rare weekends with him, why Alan was so quiet these days.

Alan thought it over.

"It's because I'm mad at you, and because I hate your stupid girlfriend … and because my mom doesn't sing anymore."

Alan expected him to get angry, but he didn't. He looked at Alan with a sadness of his own.

"I am sorry for that son, and I hope someday you'll understand."

They didn't speak of the divorce again for many years.

At home, the boys knew their mom was a proud woman and in all this time she refused to ask anyone for help, including her parents and siblings. Life settled into a routine. They were getting by, but the boys could see it was wearing their mother down.

One day Alan came home from school and Mom was asleep, which was usual with her working nights. He ventured into the kitchen to see what he could fix for dinner and maybe swing a snack.

Looking in the fridge, and in every cupboard in the kitchen, the only edible item to be found was a box of Betty Crocker chocolate cake frosting mix. Steven, just in from school behind him, joined in and they commenced to mix the frosting in a big bowl.

They were standing in the kitchen and about to start eating when Mom came out from her room. The boys greeted her casually and maintained their attention mostly to the bowl of frosting. She stood, watching them until they noticed and looked back to her.

The biggest, wettest tears either one of them had ever seen were rolling from her eyes. There was no sobbing, no movement, no sound, just tears.

"Excuse me boys, I'm sorry."

She left the living room and closed herself in the bathroom. They could hear the faucet start running, then her sobbing, almost wailing.

It broke their hearts.

The boys looked to each other. Alan was first to react.

"OK, screw this ... we need to take care of Mom."

"Yea, what are we going to do?"

Alan made a plan on the spot.

"Go and set the table with a tablecloth and candles ... everything fancy, like we do on Thanksgiving. While you do that, I'm calling Grandma."

Alan knew his mom would be furious with him for involving Grandma, but too bad. Mom was crying in front of them, and it was not OK on any level. He dialed and told his grandma what happened. She calmed his near hysteria, saying not to worry, and they would be there in about two hours.

Alan finished the call and Steven was done with the table set. They went together to the bathroom door and knocked. Their Mom opened the door and Steven spoke first.

116

"Come on Mom. We made you dinner tonight!"

She was composed and they led her to the dining table. The bowl of frosting was in the middle, between two lit candles, and crystal goblets of water, with ice cubes, were set out, along with their *fancy plates* and napkins. Steven then, in what Alan deemed a brilliant move, pulled Mom's chair out to seat her. Alan passed the bowl, with each of them scooping a helping of frosting to their plates. They ate in silence, then Alan was first to speak.

"Hey Mom, you know how at Grandma's house on Thanksgiving we go around the table and say what we're thankful for? I wanna do that, ok?"

Steven took the cue,

"Yeah! Me too!"

Alan didn't wait for a response.

"I'm thankful for having a good place to live and an ok school, and I'm grateful for having a great brother and the best mom ever."

Steven followed without a pause.

"Lord, I'm grateful for our family and friends, and we are dry and safe at night, and that our mom works so hard for us, Amen!"

Tears returned to their mom's face, but she seemed otherwise composed. The boys looked to her and after a long moment she met their gazes.

"I want you boys to know it's been the biggest blessing of my life to be your mom. I am grateful for this above all things and I'm as proud of you as I can be."

Alan flushed and, looking down at his helping of frosting, he took a bite while Mom and Steven looked on.

"Humm, tastes like chicken!"

They laughed and the tension at the table slid away. They talked and ate frosting like it was a regular meal.

Just a couple of hours later their grandma, grandpa, Aunt Renee, and their favorite cousin Sally showed up. Grandpa took charge in a relaxed way and directed the boys and Sally to go to his car and bring the rest of the groceries in. They jumped to it and were relieved to see their mom was ready to accept help.

She was chatting with her mom and sister while Sally and the boys covered the kitchen counters with bags and bags of groceries. The boys could feel their hearts warm while they stood back and watched the ladies put everything into cabinets and the fridge.

This amazing flow of goods was followed by Grandma, Aunt Renee, and Mom making an awesome spaghetti and meatball dinner, complete with salad and garlic bread, and by the time it was over, laughter and contentment was seen in them all, including Mom.

In the years following, things were never again so dire. They still needed to be frugal, but there was always food on hand and, more important, the boys saw the change it made in their mom.

Day in and day out, she was less stressed, and in fact, she seemed happier. Talking about it in hindsight, the boys saw a horrible low point for them as a turning point in their lives.

They measured their quality of life from this low benchmark, and it was a bond between them ever afterward. Blood was indeed thicker than water, and they had stuck it out together.

Icarus Falling

At 23 years old, Josh Madsen was one of the lucky ones.

He seemed to be in the right place at the right time his whole life. After joining the Air Force, right out of high school, he trained and worked for four years as a firefighter. As his enlistment neared its end, he decided he loved the notion of firefighting as a career, but he was terribly homesick. He wanted out of the service.

Taking an honorable discharge, he returned home to Port Orchard, Washington. A scant two months later, he was lucky again to land a job as a civilian firefighter on the new Navy submarine base, just up the road in Bangor.

Josh's first shift at his new job arrived and, at the 7:00 a.m. roll call, as he expected, he was called on by the captain to introduce himself to the team. He acquitted himself well when answering the crew's questions, getting his best response with their last.

"They hired you, why should we keep you?"

"Well, I'm strong … I can hump two 50-foot rolls of firehose up five floors, and not puke at the top … I'll always make you all look good and, most of all, because I have two really hot sisters … oh, and I'm such a good cook, that by next week, you won't be sure if you want to marry one of them or marry me!"

He scored big with that one. Next, he knew, the practical jokes would commence.

The complement of firefighters on duty at *Sub-Base Bangor* on any given day was eight. These teams were lean, but very efficient: A supervisory captain commanding, an engineer, two linemen, two rescue-men, and two paramedics.

As a matter of tradition, the newest team member assumed the nickname of *Probie* and all probies started as linemen. They wrestled firehoses and were on the front end of extinguishing all blazes encountered. They also got stuck doing every bit of scut work that needed doing around the station and there would be plenty of that.

After the morning roll call, Captain Manning paired Josh with the engineer, Bill Braxton, as his trainer. Bill took a relaxed approach with Josh.

"Well, welcome to the show. This here is the best gig on the planet. Here we are, milling about smartly in these chick-magnet uniforms, spending two-thirds of our day on our asses or asleep, living in this spankin' new fire palace, and picking up mega-fat paychecks every two weeks. Can it get any better?"

Bill didn't wait for an answer.

"I submit to you, it cannot!"

Josh laughed.

"Bill, I wanna stay around for sure."

"Don't worry Probie, you'll do fine. Let me run you through the routine. It's the same most every day."

Bill, with Josh in tow, led the daily inspection of Engine One, then took him on a slow tour of the entire station complex while outlining their full daily routine.

"Roll call, 7:00 a.m. sharp until 7:20. Vehicle inspections until 8:00. After that we have coffee and morning briefing with the captain until 8:30. Next, station maintenance until 10:00 ... get used to cleaning toilets and buffing floors, Probie."

Bill was clearly enjoying himself.

"Our days must be close to what you're used to from the Air Force, but one difference here is we don't go in for practical jokes, so don't do any of that here. You don't want to get off on the wrong foot."

Bill looked to his watch.

"We've got about five minutes until briefing - come on - I'll show you how to make coffee."

They went to the station's kitchen and stood before a mammoth stainless-steel, multi-pot, coffee maker.

"Everything in this station is top of the line, and commercial grade."

Bill pulled open a cabinet door.

"There's your coffee, filters, and carafes. Put a filter in the basket, three scoops of coffee, and fill your carafe at the sink. Now, this next step is very important ... flip both orange toggles on the front here *before* you pour the water into the top. Pour the water in very slowly, then set the carafe on the warmer here, got it?"

Josh nodded.

"Got it, filter first, then coffee. toggles next, then pour."

Bill nodded,

"OK Probie, get it going. Bring me a cup too. I like mine black."

Bill turned and headed to the dayroom. Josh followed Bill's instructions as the rest of the team wandered into the kitchen to grab their mugs and snacks. Josh flipped the toggles, then began to slowly pour the water into the top of the machine.

The machine started to make a hellacious gurgling racket

124

and Josh, trying to figure out what was happening, watched in horror as a thick, steady stream of hot coffee ran out of the drip basket, free falling to the warmer plate below. Josh held the carafe that was supposed to be sitting on the warmer and it was still more than half full of water.

In a panic, he set the carafe on the countertop and dashed to the cabinet for an empty carafe. The still-brewing coffee continued draining in a steady flow onto the warmer, sizzling as it boiled off. Josh shoved the empty carafe under the stream, maneuvering it into place on the warmer.

The flow of coffee, now captured, allowed Josh to take a deep breath. He looked in disbelief at the coffee dripping down the face of the cabinets and puddling on the floor. Glancing up from the disaster, Josh saw his teammates sitting at the large kitchen table watching him. His gaze was met with a hail of laughter, clapping, and whistles. He grinned sheepishly and looked at Bill.

"Rat Bastard! I thought I knew all the pranks!"

More laughter followed Josh as he stomped out of the kitchen, in mock anger, to change his coffee-splattered shirt. The pranks had begun.

The rest of the morning went fast. Station maintenance was next, then they saddled up and drove *Engine One* around on a *base familiarization tour* for a few hours. After the tour, it was back to the station for a communal lunch, then a half-hour of free time. During their break, Josh couldn't believe his luck when he saw a chance to exact revenge on Bill for the coffee maker incident.

Bill was sitting in the dayroom with a few of the other guys, watching TV, drinking a can of Coke. They were watching a rerun of a nature show which Josh coincidentally had seen a few nights previously and he knew what was about to be shown.

The narrator started talking about a two-headed snake at an Arizona roadside attraction. Josh walked up behind Bill's chair and at just the right moment, when Bill was taking in a sizable gulp of his soda, Josh leaned in and whispered,

"Gee … I wonder what those snakes do when they get mad at each other."

Bill was caught off guard by the joke and laughed explosively, causing a full stream of Coke to spray from his mouth and nostrils into the back of the chair in front of him. The rest of the team howled and clapped in appreciation of Josh's well-timed maneuver. Josh bowed in response and Bill took it with good grace.

"Alright Probie, I'll give you that was a good one - you got me."

A few minutes later, the captain announced they all were going to the *M.L.A.* for a safety briefing on Trident missiles. He then expanded for Josh's benefit.

"Gents, this is *the business end* of our business here. It's a rare opportunity for us, so let me outline how this tour is going to go … M.L.A. stands for the *Main Limited Area* and it's a highly secure 480-acre compound in the center of the base. The M.L.A. contains our Trident missiles when they are not loaded on subs. I will caution you now, there will be no screwing around of any kind during this visit."

The captain paused to let his message sink in, then continued.

"Thus far, some of you who've been here for a while have been inside the M.L.A, but none of us have been granted access to the interior of a magazine, nor been briefed on the weapons themselves. That is changing today. We will be in the presence of nuclear weapons, and we will learn what our role is in protecting them from fire."

Josh didn't know Captain Manning very well yet, but he could tell the man was being earnest. Manning continued.

"Guarding the M.L.A. is the 68th Marine Corp Security Force Company … these are real Marines … the cream of the crop, with real bullets and real orders to kill anyone even thinking about molesting their missiles."

Josh was aware there were nuclear weapons on the base, but didn't know much more about them, and he hadn't thought about it to this point. Captain Manning posed a question.

"These Marines … do you know what their motto is? It's embroidered on their Company battle flag in their headquarters building … *Mors de Contactus* … for those of you who don't speak Latin, that translates to *Death on Contact.*"

Manning drew a breath and shuddered.

"I mean really, *Death on Contact?* … Christ almighty! You jokers are not to play with these guys, even a little bit, do you understand?"

With that, the team mounted their trucks and Bill filled Josh in more.

"Cap is right, those Marines will tear your head off, bare-handed, and piss down the hole in your neck if you even blink wrong at one of those missiles. As for myself, I sleep better knowing they're on it, all day, every day. These guys are wound tight. They only relax once a year, on Christmas Eve, for about two minutes."

Before Josh could ask what that meant, Bill continued.

"It's the damnedest thing. We share an emergency radio channel with the Base Shore Patrol and the Marines, and at midnight last Christmas Eve, a bunch of Marines started squawking on the channel about seeing an incoming UFO. They described a big, red, flying sleigh, eight reindeer, and a sleigh pilot wearing a red suit ... they gave estimated speed, direction of travel, and asked for clearance to attack the UFO.

Kilo One, Kilo 12, we have a target lock with two surface-to-airs, request permission to smoke this fat slob, over. All kinds of radio transmissions like that, for about a minute until one of the officers gets on the radio and tells them all *'Shut the hell up and get back to work'*. It's the only bit of screwing around I've seen out of them in my 15 months working here."

Josh tried to imagine the scene, then his thoughts drifted as they rolled toward the M.L.A. He reviewed in his mind what he knew about *nukes*, then he thought about being called in if a missile caught fire.

These things have safety redundancy out the ass, like that B-52 crash with nukes onboard in Arkansas a few years ago. Four of the bombs slammed into the ground and burned up without detonating ... but they weren't sitting on top of rocket fuel either. Well hell, look at this base though ... all the safety everywhere you look, the Navy is positively nuts about it. I'd put the odds of a nuke being involved in a fire on this base at next to none.

Their fire truck rolled on and Josh turned his attention to their surroundings. They were beautiful. The Olympic Peninsula sat amid a lush coastal rain forest, with tens of thousands of pines and redwoods, some 40, some 50 feet tall, infusing the air with the smell of … life. The base itself was situated at the edge of the Hood Canal, where the behemoth Ohio class Subs came and went from the Pacific Ocean.

Josh appreciated being surrounded by nature, even with all the new buildings and ongoing construction on the base. The forest gave his workplace a distinctive park-like feel. He took in a deep, satisfying, breath of the chilled spring air and then he saw it … The M.L.A. His pulse quickened.

Showtime! Let's get in here and find out what's what!

Their convoy of three fire vehicles stopped at the fortified gate complex blocking the road. A 12-foot-high chain-link fence with wicked-looking coils of razor wire crowning it, stretched off from either side of the gate. The gate itself was the first of two. Josh saw the complex created a holding pen for vehicles entering the M.L.A. The first gate slid open, and their

Fire Engine inched in, stopping in front of the still closed second gate, while the first gate closed behind them.

They were in the enclosed yard with a small, four-season, guard shack and, most remarkably, a half-dozen U.S. Marines in battle fatigues looking positively intimidating with their strapped-on M-16s and sidearms. The other two fire vehicles were still outside the first gate waiting. Josh guessed correctly the procedure was for vehicles to be admitted to the M.L.A. only one at a time.

Wow, this is some tight security!

One of the Marines stood back from the rest. He held a leashed German Shepard. Both the Marine and the Shepard were watching the truck and its occupants in silence. Two other Marines each held six-foot poles with plate-sized search mirrors attached at the ends. Another Marine stood a little further back, with his M-16 held at a *Low Ready* position, watching the entire scene. Two more Marines were in the guard shack and one of them stepped out. He came over to the truck and greeted them formally.

"Gentlemen, good afternoon. We have been briefed on your purpose for being here and you are to be admitted. Please step down and form a line at the guard shack, with your ID cards in hand."

The firefighters complied and, as they moved toward the shack, Josh saw the canine handler and Marines with search mirrors move in on their rig. They started searching every nook, cranny, and compartment of the vehicle with practiced thoroughness.

The Marine who'd greeted them, a lieutenant, looked the group over and then spoke to Captain Manning, the first in line.

"Badge, please. State your name, date of birth, and Social Security number."

The captain complied. The Marine held the ID picture up near the captain's face, compared the two, then flipped the card over to verify the captain's response.

"Wait here."

The Marine carried the captain's ID into the guard shack. Josh saw through the windows that there was a large board on the wall inside the shack with about 90 ID cards hanging from it. The Marine located the captain's card on the board and compared the two. Bill, in a hushed tone, filled Josh in.

"He's matching code numbers in the upper corner of our ID cards with the cards kept in that shack. The numbers must match. Those badges on the board represent the only civilians who are allowed to enter the M.L.A. If you present an ID without a companion on that board, or if your code number doesn't match your card in the shack, these Marines will stomp mudholes in you and drag what's left to the brig, and that's if you don't resist … If you resist, well, they will just friggin' kill you … and don't think I'm kidding."

Josh boggled at this and didn't say anything. Bill continued.

"These six Jarheads here are just the ones we see. There are about two dozen others watching us right now through binoculars and on surveillance cameras. They are *camo'ed* up and dug into the woods, sporting .50 caliber machine guns, sniper rifles, mortars, shoulder-fired missiles. You name it. I kid you not. Twenty-four hours a day, 365 days a year, these killers are praying for an assault on this place. Welcome Probie, to the safest place on earth."

Josh looked to the surrounding woods, then back to the shack.

Holy Hell! What am I getting myself into?

The Marine handed Captain Manning his ID badge back.

"You can pass sir. Please return to your vehicle and wait for your companions."

And so it went, each firefighter in turn was scrutinized and directed back to the firetruck. When all were again back onboard, the Marine officer spoke to Bill.

"Pull through and stop to wait behind that pickup truck up ahead. Your other firetrucks will be along shortly."

Bill nodded, drove past the second gate, and stopped about a hundred yards further up, behind a pickup occupied by two more armed Marines. The second gate closed behind them.

Josh's head was spinning a little and he looked at the captain as they waited.

"Hey Cap, we are going live through this briefing, right?"

The captain cracked a smile.

"Don't worry Josh, this is just another day at the office."

After a time, they were joined by the rest of their team. One of the Marines in the pickup was speaking on a handheld radio. The Marine then approached them and gave driving instructions to Bill.

"Sir, please follow behind me. Do not pass me or stop your truck for any reason."

The Marine looked the group over and continued,

"None of you are permitted to exit this vehicle until we arrive at the magazine you are assigned to visit today. Am I understood?"

He was understood.

It was a short drive to one of the many magazines, which all looked the same, like buried overgrown Quonset huts. Flat-faced, with heavy-duty steel doors and large sod-covered earthen mounds over them. The magazines were fronted by very large circular driveways. The Marine pickup led them to the front of one of them and parked.

The team cautiously dismounted their vehicles and a Navy lieutenant, emerging from inside the *hut,* approached them.

"Welcome gentlemen, I'm Lieutenant Gene Steadman, but you can call me Max."

Max seemed relaxed in comparison to the Marines.

"I am the missile control officer on the U.S.S. *Tennessee,* which you've no doubt seen presently berthed down at the wharf. We're going to go in here in a minute, take a real good look at the missile inside, and answer what questions we can for you. First though, a few reminders. Any unauthorized photography or making artistic renderings of any kind, of any part of the M.L.A., are federal crimes. It is likewise a crime to make any video or audio recording of any portion of this briefing, and finally, it would be a criminal violation for you to communicate what is discussed and seen here today, with any unauthorized person."

Max let a silence lay between them.

"You are here only because if, somehow, it ever happens one of these missiles catches fire, you'll need to know what will, and what won't happen as a consequence."

Max stopped for a moment and let another pause build.

"I'll tell you two things at the start. One; with all the safety precautions built into these devices, from the magazine storage protocols, to the loading of the birds at the explosives handling wharf, it is extraordinarily unlikely one will ever be involved in a fire. The second thing I will say is this. If one of these missiles *is* ever involved in a fire, I pity you poor bastards. Come on in, I'm feeling up to scaring the hell out of you today."

The team moved inside the magazine and Josh looked at the space itself, intentionally ignoring the missile at the far end for the moment. The magazine's interior was a solid-looking concrete dome, about 20 feet to the top. It was near 50 feet wide and ran back to about 100 feet deep.

Lighting and fire-protection sprinkler pipes ran the length of the ceiling, as well as a set of tracks for a large, built-in crane specially made to handle missiles. The space was well-lit and ventilated, with a set of additional pipes and cables running down each side wall to provide the *hut* with water and power for several workbenches.

136

The team moved with Max toward the back, where their attention was drawn to ... *It.*

Two Navy missile technicians, working inside an open panel on the side of the missile, ignored the group. The missile lay sideways, cradled in an enormous custom-made rack, across the back of the space, gleaming in the powerful overhead LED lighting. Josh's breath caught in his throat, and he stared at the missile, wide-eyed.

The team, gathering in a semi-circle about six feet away, was quiet and waited for Max to continue.

"It is public knowledge the United States government entered the cold war with the Soviet Union and soon adopted a policy of nuclear deterrence called Triade. Triade consists of three components; first is an Air Force ground force of networked nuclear missile silos. Second is an Air Force component of a whole crapload of nuclear armed B-52 Stratofortress bombers, and lastly, there is this third component, the Navy's two fleets of nuclear missile submarines. One fleet is based in the Atlantic, at Kings Bay, Georgia, and the other based here, for the Pacific."

Max made eye contact with each of them as he spoke.

"Any one of these three components could, by itself, destroy life as we know it on this entire planet within about an

137

hour and a half of launch. Together, they create a surety of retribution so terrible that no sane government would contemplate risking such a war with us, and that is mad … M.A.D. - *mutually assured destruction*. The MAD strategy is at the heart of our national defense. All of this is public knowledge."

Max smiled at the team, then continued.

"What the public does not know are the practical details of the *Triade Doctrine*. You, gentleman, have a need to know *some* of these practical details, so here we go."

The team maintained their silence, giving Max rapt attention.

"For the Navy's part, here is what you need to know about the most lethal and secret weapons in the world. This spawn of Satan, laying innocently before you, is a U. S. Navy D-5 submarine-launched missile. It is more commonly known as the Trident II. This particular missile is named *Sandy*. I named her this because I met a Sandy once in high school. Sandy was the meanest, toughest, bitch I ever knew. She seduced my heart one day, and the next, she took it, stuffed it in a blender, hit the *frappe* button, and laughed while walking away. I was depressed for weeks afterwards just thinking about that girl. This Sandy makes me feel the same … only worse."

Max's vision had the men laughing nervously and he motioned them to come in and stand closer.

"Sandy here is designed for launch from an Ohio-class submarine and to carry a W-88 thermonuclear warhead. Sandy will fly on a suborbital path of up to 7,500 nautical miles from her launch point. She will then deliver her payload of eight separate warheads, within one city block of anywhere on the planet designated by the President of the United States, so ... purely as a side note ... I beg you, think about this little factoid the next time you vote."

Max paused, pacing his remarks, to give the team time to keep up with his descriptions of the weapons program.

"The W-88 warhead holds eight independently targetable nuclear bombs which provide a yield of 475 Kilotons each. These are, in fact, the most powerful warheads in the U.S. arsenal. For the sake of perspective, compare *one* of these eight bombs, to the bomb used on Hiroshima, which yielded 15 Kilotons. For those of you who are dunces, just one of these bombs is equal to 32 Hiroshima bombs ... and each missile carries eight of them."

Max was pacing slowly in front of the team as he lectured. The shop lights bejeweled the brass and ribbons of his dress whites, adding to the effect of his melodic voice. The men were mesmerized.

"On any given day, 1.2 miles from this magazine, at the explosives handling wharf, there can be as many as 24 of these missiles being loaded, or unloaded, onto a single submarine. Shall we do the math again? That's eight warheads per missile, times 24 missiles, totaling 192 warheads, or an explosive capability of just over 92 Megatons … or 6,080 Hiroshima bombs … on one submarine … concentrated into about the same square footage as your average bowling alley. Now I ask you, what could possibly go wrong?"

Max paused while the team low-whistled and murmured in response.

"I cannot tell you how happy I am you gents are here today and here is why. The Ohio-class sub is virtually undetectable at sea, and we have 14 of them in service between the two fleets."

Max paused again, setting an evenly paced rhythm for his briefing.

"Because of this, I am very sure the Russians do not want to mess with us. The prospect of nuclear war isn't what keeps me up at night. What does keep me up, and is a much more likely scenario, is for Sandy, or one of her evil sisters, to be involved in a handling accident and catch fire."

Josh, enthralled, watched as the missile technicians finished removing bolts from the nosecone of the missile. Max nodded to them, giving permission to pull the nosecone forward, exposing the eight conical nuclear warheads inside for viewing. Josh saw how the third-stage rocket motor fuel tank protruded into the center of the confined space and how it was surrounded by the warheads, each about six feet long and two feet wide at their base. They were matte black, yet gleaming.

Jumping freaking Jesus! This thing is real? Am I really here, seeing this?

A wave of nausea and faintness washed over him, but he stood his ground. The technicians withdrew and Max steepled his fingers to his lips in thought.

"First, there is some good news. The chances of an accidental full nuclear chain reaction from one of these bombs is zero. The engineers and scientists at Lockheed-Martin and at Sandia Labs have been safety testing them for years, dropping them from cranes and planes, and burning them up. There are several classified features of the arming mechanisms which make an accidental chain reaction impossible."

Josh felt a brief bit of relief.

"The bad news is this. You have four major safety concerns here as firefighters.

One - the Trident is a 44-foot long, three-stage rocket, holding about 110,000 pounds of solid powder fuel, clad only in a thin epoxy–graphite skin for weight reduction.

Two - the solid fuel, by design, is a highly energetic, but also highly explosive, class 1.1 propellant.

Three - The eight warheads on each missile, again by design, are wrapped around the solid fuel tank for the third stage rocket, with no separation.

Four - There are a classified number of pounds of high explosive in each warhead, used to create the implosion needed to start a nuclear chain reaction. It is a highly unstable, plastic explosive composite."

Max paused.

"The weapon was constrained in design by the absolute need for miniaturization, weight reduction, range, speed, and explosive power. So again, just in case there are any dunces among you, let me summarize. You will be in proximity to a massive, thin walled, plastic tube, filled with 55 tons of explosive rocket fuel, which will be burning into a huge, heaping pile of unstable plastic explosives, surrounding an unshielded core of a classified number of pounds of weapons-

142

grade plutonium. Again, I ask you … what could possibly go wrong?"

Max stood holding his hands behind his back, looking at the team.

"In the event of a high-explosive detonation of one of these missiles, without a chain reaction, which is what we would expect, the nuclear material would be dispersed over a large area. Enough radioactive material would be spread to kill tens of thousands of people after floating across Puget Sound and settling, most likely, in Seattle. Radiation sickness and cancer deaths by the thousands would follow in the path of the prevailing winds, going on for years afterwards. This would occur after the immediate explosion. Hundreds of people on this base and in Silverdale and in Poulsbo, would be killed in the initial explosion … and they'd be the lucky ones."

Max, still holding his hands behind his back, looked down, as if deep in thought.

"Here is the truth of it. If you are on duty and a fire starts involving a Trident, and if you can't put that fire out before the rocket fuel, or the high explosive in the war heads detonate, the plutonium cores inside each warhead will be blown apart. This would be a grave problem gentleman. Imagine this explosion creating a crater 400 feet across, and 40 feet deep … it would flatten half of this base and break windows as far as twenty miles away in Bremerton. If you are on duty that day, and by some miracle you're not killed outright by the blast, you'll be squirting water onto the flames of what's left until you collapse from acute radiation exposure, meaning until you simultaneously crap and vomit up a couple buckets of blood, then drop dead. It's *game over* before you start. You fellows are not here to render the nukes safe … there is no *safe* for these missiles once their fuel catches fire."

Max was winding down.

"All of this is assuming of course the accident involves only one missile. I have a confession. I've determined, after much thought that I, with only one brain, don't have enough mental capacity to imagine how much worse of a shit-show would result if a missile exploded with other missiles adjacent to it, say while being loaded onto a sub for example. So, there you have it … are there any questions I can answer?"

After a long pause, Josh half raised his hand.

"Can I touch it?"

Max broke a grin.

"Sure thing Icarus, knock yourself out."

Josh didn't know who Icarus was, but he took Max's answer as a *yes.* He stepped up, raised his hand to one of the warheads, and touched it.

It was smooth … and warm. He felt the weapon vibrating, very slightly, and in that moment, he was sure it was alive, with a malevolent will of its own.

It was horrifyingly beautiful, and he was in awe of it as he hated it. Josh dropped his hand and stepped back. He looked again at Max.

"Who is Icarus?"

"Greek mythology, look it up and you'll understand. Any other questions?"

No one spoke. The briefing was over.

The team made an orderly exit from the magazine and mounted their vehicles. Josh was relieved to be leaving.

'Shit show' is right Max. How can anyone even sleep thinking about this stuff?

Josh was done with it. He craved getting away from the M.L.A. and back to the relaxed pace of the evening hours at the firehouse.

Back on Engine One, none of the four men said anything as they drove. Josh understood this. He himself was reeling from the information they'd been given. He couldn't help trying to visualize the blast effects on the buildings and scenery he was looking at as they wound their way back.

The workday was over.

The team, back at the station, were in the kitchen fixing dinner and setting the table. They were all quiet at first, but then began to talk, almost hesitantly at first. Josh was glad to see that they too were affected. They talked about it together all through their meal.

After dinner, and doing dishes, Josh kept thinking about the comment Max made.

Who is Icarus? I have to know.

Flopping down into one of the big stuffed chairs in the dayroom he dug his cell phone out of his pocket and tapped up his Wikipedia app.

Let's see what the gospel according to Wiki has to say.

He typed in *Icarus* and read:

> *… from Greek mythology - The craftsman Daedalus, and his son Icarus, were imprisoned by King Minos in the palace tower. Over time, Daedalus managed to create two sets of wings of feathers, glued together with wax.*

Daedalus taught Icarus how to fly. He then warned Icarus not to fly too high and near to the Sun, which would cause the wax to melt, nor too low, which would cause the feathers to get wet with sea water.

Together, they escaped the tower and Icarus, overjoyed, soon forgot his father's warnings. Flying higher and higher as they fled, Icarus had come too close to the Sun. His wings dissolved and he fell into the sea and drowned.

Josh thought he got Max's meaning.

Josh was like Icarus, but was he saying to Josh to pay attention and be careful to not get too close to the bomb?

No ... it's even simpler. He just meant be careful because I was getting too close to danger. Good advice I'd say.

Josh sighed and tucked his phone back into his pocket. He turned his attention to the TV and tried to forget about Tridents ... and Icarus.

———————

At the same moment Josh had been tucking his phone back into his pocket, 3.2 miles away at the explosives handling wharf, Seaman Jeffery Hastings was scrambling to finish the task at hand. He was straddling the nosecone of a W-88 warhead atop a Trident missile, inside a silo on the deck of the USS

Tennessee. The missile wasn't Sandy, but it was one of her evil sisters. He had just secured the last lifting strap to the nosecone for the crane to lift the missile from the silo, and then slide it into its transport container on the waiting semi-trailer. The trailer would then haul the missile a whopping 0.8 miles up the slope from the canal to the M.L.A., where the missile would be deposited in one of the magazines for maintenance and storage.

Hastings, a missile handling technician, had done this task of securing a Trident for lifting more than 80 times during his newly minted career.

He was part of a five-man handling team and his four partners had just started walking off the dock for a break.

The team consisted of two missile techs - himself and Seaman Anthony Watkins. Next, a crane operator - Machinists Mate Eric Tobias, and a fourth member of the team was a semi-truck driver - Yeoman Ray Goodall (He hauled the missiles back and forth between the dock and the M.L.A.). Rounding out the team, was their supervisor - Chief Petty Officer Raphael Campos.

Hastings lagged, but only long enough to finish threading a bolt through a lifting strap. He finished and scurried up the six-foot ladder used to get them down inside the submarine's launch tubes. He was anxious to catch up to his

148

team because safety protocol demanded the two technicians come and go together whenever an operation was in progress.

All Missile Handling Team members knew the drill. When removing a missile from a silo, two missile technicians had to be present in the well of the silo. They were to secure four straps, lowered from the crane, onto the four lifting hard points at the base of the missile's nosecone. They each would attach two of the straps, using inch and a half thick, grade 8 bolts and then they were to double-check each other's work. This done, they were to climb out of the silo, one behind the other, with the last one out hauling the ladder up behind him.

On this occasion, Hastings was last out ... but he didn't bring out the ladder.

He wasn't lazy, or dumb ... he just made the most basic of human mistakes. He allowed himself to be distracted. He was concerned at that moment about breaking a different rule by not staying together with his team. He simply forgot the ladder.

About 20 minutes later their break was over and Campos directed the team to head back to the sub to finish the lift. They ambled back and took up positions for the crane lift.

The accident was inevitable now.

It hadn't been any one thing. It was several things, in a perfect storm. Hastings forgot the ladder ... Watkins should have waited for Hastings to check his work and exit the silo, verifying the ladder got pulled out with them ... Tobias and Woodall both should have noticed Hastings and Watkins' lapse in protocol and sounded off ... and Campos, who also should have noticed the lapse, additionally failed to be the safety net, and visually inspect the well of the silo prior to the lift.

If any one of these five small steps were executed, the accident would have been prevented. But they weren't ... and none of them noticed the lapse.

They were in their assigned spots for the lift, and no one could see that the ladder was still down in the well of the silo. Campos radioed the team for an *all clear,* and all responded with an *affirmative.*

Tobias engaged the crane and began lifting the missile from the narrow confines of the silo. The ladder rose upward on the lip of the nosecone, scraping along the side of the silo for about three feet. The top of the ladder then hit the hatch-ring at the top of the silo, trapping it. The missile continued the rise and the ladder collapsed with the force of the lift, causing one of its feet to puncture the thin, plastic skin of the missile hull.

The missile continued rising, flattening the ladder between the wall of the silo and the skin of the missile. The foot of the ladder punched through the sidewall skin of the missile, as easily as a knife through butter, as it continued lifting upward.

The scraping sound created by the damage didn't register with anyone watching the lift for several seconds. Several more seconds were lost in stopping the lift when Campos blurted into his radio for Tobias to stop the crane.

The top 15 feet of the missile showed above the silo now, and the team saw the gapping slice in the missile hull. Powdered rocket fuel poured out of the rip in the hull at hundreds of pounds per second, spilling onto the sub deck and dock. Like sand running out of a broken hourglass, the powder fell and created an expanding cloud, creeping along the length of the sub and the wharf.

Hastings, near the bow of the sub, was stunned. He could see and smell the rocket fuel washing over them and he looked, wide-eyed, with his mouth hanging open. Campos was yelling for help into his radio and everything else seemed to be at a standstill. Hastings didn't know what to do … looking around for anything to help, his gaze set upon the dock pole holding the sub-tender bundle.

This bundle supplied water, communication cables, and electric power to the sub while it was berthed. Hastings realized there was a danger of the power connection igniting the powdery cloud of rocket fuel gathering around them.

The fuel, continuing to cascade from the missile, had created a fog so thick that Hastings could barely see the sub next to him by now, and his lungs began to burn with each breath. He sprinted to the power bundle, fearing he'd soon collapse. He reached the pole and saw the two 440-volt power cords running from the sub to a large gray control box with a large red handle, secured to the post on the wharf. There was no time. The fuel could be detonated by the electric current at any moment.

Without further thought, he yanked both power cables from the sockets, cutting off the power to the sub.

Hasting's bravery was the final act in this perfect storm. When he pulled the power cords, the connections arced, creating open sparks as the live current chased the metal prongs being pulled from the live sockets.

If Hastings had only slammed down the red power supply handle instead, the arc would have been contained in the safety of the box … But he hadn't … And the two arcs of bare electricity immediately ignited the fuel cloud around them.

In milliseconds, the entirety of the rocket fuel load exploded, with the predicted explosive force of 155,000 tons of TNT.

In the next few following moments, the exploding missile nearly vaporized the USS Tennessee ... and the eight other missiles remaining on board.

The fuel from those eight missiles, in turn, then exploded at once ...

There wasn't anyone left, for many miles, and for many weeks afterward, who could do that math.

———————

At the instant this explosion occurred, Josh, who had finally distracted himself from his grim thoughts about Tridents and Icarus, was watching TV and joking with his fellow firefighters. They were all startled by a sudden brilliant flash of white light through the station's large dayroom windows ... but they didn't have time to understand what it was.

The rocket fuel and high explosives from nine fully fueled and armed Trident missiles, 3.2 miles away from them, burst ... brighter than the Sun.

All the firemen, including Josh, immediately died in the explosion.

At 23 years old, Josh Madsen ... once again it turned out ... was one of the lucky ones.

Not to Be

Rose Jamison was ill … she was very ill, and she had to come to grips with it.

Making her way from her pulmonologist's office toward her car, she was wondering just then if she could even finish the short trek.

Dr. Max Bedard had diagnosed her a year before. *Alpha-One Antitrypsin Deficiency,* he had told her then, was an incurable and hereditary form of emphysema and he had taken her through what she could expect with the progression of the disease.

It was grim and the months had unfolded much as he had warned her. She was still working but had, just today during her appointment, agreed with him she couldn't do it anymore. She was on portable oxygen now all the time and she just had nothing left in terms of the will to fight on.

Only she would ever know it, but the walk from the doctor's office to her car on that visit was the worst moment she had ever had to push through in her life.

For her, it represented the end of her independence and the start of her final chapter … it scared her some and it made her angry.

She reached her car, a newish Toyota, let the shoulder strap of her small oxygen canister slip down and set the contraption on the pavement. When she opened her car door, a strong odor of urine wafted into her face from the hot interior, and she frowned.

Just another indignity. I can't even drive anymore without pissing myself.

Rose was 47, long divorced with two sons, grown but living nearby, for which she was grateful. She lived alone in a nice house with a pool she never used and her primary occupation, other than her job, was being in the midst of a pointless affair with her married boss for over three years.

She knew he would never leave his wife and, she had to admit to herself, she preferred it that way. She had always been independent and didn't want to muck her life up again with any man, after working so hard for so many years to have created a safe and comfortable existence for herself. The only other preoccupations in her life were the four real soft spots in her heart: Her two sons, and her two grandchildren.

Rose sat in her car with the door open, struggling to catch her breath for a minute, then she hauled the oxygen canister in behind her. Exhausted from the small walk, she still couldn't yet muster the energy to start her car and drive.

Damn it! I hate this ... and what's worse? I want a cigarette so bad that I can taste it!

It was as obvious to Rose as it was to anyone else, nobody should smoke if they had Emphysema. But what could she say? She was addicted.

It was one of her few shames, the way friends and strangers alike, looked at her when she smoked. She pictured herself sitting there, next to her oxygen canister, barely able to draw light inhales from a cigarette after maneuvering her oxygen cannula out of the way of her lips.

What a pathetic sight I must be ... well, this too shall pass soon enough.

Rose stared out the windshield and thought about all the things she needed to do to adjust to her changing life. The beginning of the end of her life. She sighed as a few tears rolled from the corners of her eyes, and she lit up a smoke.

The next two months were very busy for Rose. She had *retired* from the bank, filed for disability, ended her affair, and acclimated herself to a new lightweight wheelchair. She also sold her house (after a massive downsizing of personal property), and she, with her few remaining belongings, moved in with her youngest son Matt and his young family.

She was adapting to life in her son's home, and she attributed it to being free of property and responsibility … and to being around her grandkids every day.

Rose acknowledged one other reason she was adapting so well to her new lifestyle. Matt's wife, Polly, had made extraordinary efforts to integrate her into their household. Polly was peerless in the basic care she provided Rose, and she kept Rose engaged in productive and fun projects and activities daily.

All was well for a time. But time, as it does, rolled on and life changed again. A day came when Matt received a career-making job offer from out of state. Rose was supportive of the notion, and she was very matter of fact in discussing the move.

"I, of course, will be staying behind. My friends and the rest of my family are here, and well, there's Dr. Bedard. I can't start over again with another doctor."

They all knew her brave face was crap, but they also knew Rose would not, and could not, adjust to life elsewhere. There was nothing to be done, so nothing more was said about it. She was staying.

Rose's boys moved her into a nice four-plex apartment. They unpacked her belongings, stocked her cabinets, and got her situated. Matt's family moved and, as a part of the plan, Mike, her oldest son, stepped in. Mike deemed himself a poor substitute for Matt and Polly, but he dedicated himself to providing adequate, if not stellar, attention to his mom.

Divorced himself, with no children, it was easy for him to move to an apartment three blocks away from Rose's new place the same month.

Mike, a police officer, worked a 7 p.m. to 3 a.m. shift, with Wednesdays and Thursdays off. This steady schedule, and some good communication with a few of her neighbors, led to Rose being well covered should she need anything.

As he soon discovered, Rose needed help with almost everything. Though she could walk, she had to have a wheelchair always when out of the house because even a few steps would wipe her out. She had given up driving by then. She didn't have the strength to get her wheelchair on and off the car rack, so Mike realized he was it.

He soon found he was much more involved in her doings than he had expected, but it had turned out he enjoyed hanging with her more than he thought he would.

Rose was a positive person by nature, with a hilarious wit, and she was an engaging person to be around. She and Mike had always had a close rapport and shared a lot of common interests.

159

When together, they spent time *watching* TV with the volume almost too low to hear. They would talk for hours about books, movies, art, philosophy, poetry, history, politics, and world affairs. Being influenced by his mom all his life, it was no surprise they almost always found themselves in agreement on things and when they weren't, she had the uncanny ability to bring him around to her way of thinking like nobody he ever knew.

Rose accomplished this by way of just a few insightful questions about his position on a given topic and in effect got him to change his opinion based on how he answered her, not on persuasive arguments from her. He just loved this about her.

When they were 'talked out', they would read together in companionable silence. Sometimes when reading, they would call for each other's attention and read aloud some interesting passage from something. Rose was fond of reading him passages from a tome of Shakespeare, which she kept near at hand to her customary sitting spot. A point of pride for Mike was, though he thought himself bright, he was positive his mom was smarter.

Though physically limited, Rose still loved going places and seeing people. Mike had keyed in on this as a morale booster for her. On most workdays, Mike would be off duty and

160

home to sleep about 4:00 a.m. He'd wake at about10:30 and by 11:00 he'd be showered, dressed, and over to Mom's place.

But Wednesdays every week were special. Wednesdays were *Mall Day*. He would come over, load her and the wheelchair into his SUV, and they'd drive to the mall. Once there, Mike would roll her in, guiding the chair from behind, and they'd shop for a few hours.

They began their outings by taking the elevator up to the top level. Mike would guide Rose past every shop and stop at those she directed. Once the circuit of the top floor had been covered, they took the elevator down and repeated the process on the lower floor.

Along the way Rose would engage people by cuing in on what they were buying or something at hand of mutual interest. She was skilled at this in fact and Mike was amazed at how many people opened-up to her and chatted with her like old friends. It took Mike a few Wednesdays to catch on, but the casual conversations Rose got into were part of a game she had developed between her son and herself.

Rose would go out of her way to spot, then get near any attractive woman within eyeshot. She would feign interest in anything near to where the woman would be, and she'd have

Mike wheel her over. Next, Rose would see something she *just had to look at* and ask Mike to inch her in.

Rose would start chatting with the woman, asking her opinion on a garment, or commenting on something the woman had and, in short order, they were in a full-blown chat. Midway in these chats, Rose would introduce the woman to her dutiful son, slipping in the facts he was a policeman, and single.

Rose was shamelessly convincing in these encounters and Mike could only watch and control his occasional urges to laugh out loud. He didn't need his mom's help *finding a nice girl*, but he took it with good grace, smiled, and went with it.

Whenever Rose concluded one of these *chance meetings*, she would share her assessment of the woman's character, demeanor, and ability to bring forth grandchildren to her. Mike always ended up laughing as she did so because she made her comments with an analytical detachment which he knew she wasn't really exercising.

She was just having fun with him and the notion of finding him the right girl. She'd then solicit Mike's impressions of the woman, knowing this would lead them into their weekly discussion on the state of his love life and when he was planning on settling down … to raise kids … the only part of the entire farce she was interested in.

On rare occasion Rose would buy something in one of the shops, but more often they ended their outings without any purchases and their last stop was always at the coffee shop at the mall entrance. The food was good there and their habit was to drink coffee and talk for a long time after eating. For dessert, they always split a piece of pie, more to extend their chat than any need to satisfy a sweet tooth.

Life went on in this way and Mike continued supporting Rose's independence as best he could. But again, in the fullness of time, the decline in Rose's health had drained her of both her energy, and her joy in life. At times Mike noticed she struggled just to breathe when sitting still at home.

Mike had been with her to doctor's appointments many times before and he was accustomed to her preference he remain in the waiting room. One such day however, she surprised him. She asked him to come to the examination room with her. The doctor soon joined them and introduced himself to Mike.

Dr. Bedard turned his attention to Rose, and they greeted each other. Bedard was holding her limp hands with a confident reassurance. He took her pulse and counted her respirations while asking her questions. Mike noticed how he spent a very long time listening to Rose's breathing with his stethoscope.

Bedard was about Mike's age, and he seemed earnest and compassionate. He treated Rose with a tenderness unusual for a doctor, in Mike's opinion, and he found himself liking the doctor very much. Mike listened in silence as they talked about her medication dosages and Bedard's wish he could do more for her.

Rose and Mike left the office. On the ride home he asked why she had invited him in this time.

"It's a bit complicated and I will explain later, but I just need to have you involved and understanding where I stand. A better answer will have to wait for a bit."

Mike accepted this and he went in with her to her next two appointments. Over the span of just a few months Mike became more concerned. He saw his mom lose energy and struggle harder and harder for every breath. It was clear to him she was terminally ill. Rose seemed as if she had been robbed of hope and she looked weary ... more than he had ever seen in her before.

On a day in September, they were at another appointment. Dr. Bedard broached a subject not included in their prior visits.

"Rose, I can see you're struggling more to breath, and I know this often leads to a deep depression. I've seen it in my

164

other patients. I want to prescribe a medication to ease this for you."

Bedard had scratched out a script while he had been talking and handed it to her.

"There are also other things which can help, like support groups and psychological counseling. Look through this literature with Mike and you two can tailor an approach to deal with what you're experiencing."

Bedard was clinical in his demeanor, yet he was gentle with her at the same time. He put his hand on Rose's forearm.

"I know this is hard, and you're tired, and we've talked about how this disease progresses. I want you to start thinking about conserving your energy and staying home and resting more than you have been."

Mike had a sick feeling hearing these words. He was reading between the lines and was sure Bedard was leading her to think about preparing for the end of her life.

They left the office, both a little frightened. Things were changing. Instead of heading for the car like usual, Rose asked Mike to take a detour to the center of an outdoor courtyard of the medical complex. The weather was pleasant, and they settled in a quiet, shaded area near a small fountain.

Mike sat on a cement bench facing her. She seemed so frail to him, sitting in her wheelchair, and for a long minute neither spoke. Rose rolled her chair in close to him and reached for his hand and held it. He held her gaze and waited for her to speak. She looked at him, offered a weak smile, and began.

"You know, I've had a pretty wonderful life. My childhood was not one bit short of grand and I even loved being a teenager. I was a typical and happy girl growing up, and then I became a mother. It wasn't until then I knew what real happiness was."

Mike was having trouble maintaining eye contact with Rose for fear he'd start blubbering and he glanced away saying,

"Well, Matt and I are biased, but you're the best mom ever … just saying."

Rose smiled and gripped his hand just a little bit tighter. "Charmer."

She didn't say anything else at first. She just continued to smile at him.

"I want to tell you just some of the many wonderful things I remember about you boys and the joy you've brought me."

Rose brightened as she looked into Mike's eyes.

"Do you want to know about the happiest day of my entire life? Have I ever told you about this?"

Mike was caught off guard by the force and determination with which his mother was guiding their conversation.

"No, I don't believe you have."

"You were five and a half and Matty was four. We were living inland still, in Gardena, and neither of you had ever been to the beach. Your dad was working, but his mother, your Grandma Francis, was with us and I packed all four of us up for a day at the beach. I'm fortunate I've always loved my mother-in-law, so it made this day special from the beginning. We drove to the beach, and I had you boys singing songs on the way, and it was a beautiful day."

Rose smiled, looking off into the distance, and continued.

"I can remember it all, the smell of salt air as we got close, and the excitement you and Matty showed on your first glimpse of the ocean."

Mike remembered this day too. He had never mentioned it to her, but it was one of his favorite days as well. Rose continued,

167

"We got our blankets and baskets and went down to the sand. I could hardly keep either of you from running straight into the waves. I told you both not to go into the water past your waist and tried to get you two to sit still long enough for some Coppertone, but you were too excited. I had to give up and let you go. You both went in the water, past your waists, straight off and Grandma Francis laughed herself silly watching me in a panic, trying to corral you both. She told me it was like watching someone trying to get cats to march in a parade."

Rose was looking off into the distance, beaming at the memory of her own story. She paused for a moment and looked back to Mike.

"You two swam and had waves knocking you down, one after another, and you both were laughing the whole time. The joy of seeing my two boys experience pure fun of their own sent me to a place of happiness and peace I'd never been to before. It was even better than when you were born because you both were aware, engaging the world, and loving it."

Mike remembered this and how, later in the day, they had walked up the beach a long way until they came to some tide pools. He asked Rose if she recalled it, and she did.

"Son, I remember everything about that day. It was the most magical day of my life. Matty found a big bright-orange starfish and you found a rather large hermit crab. You two would have stayed there until dark if I hadn't pulled you away. After the beach, do you remember what we did next?"

Mike thought on it but couldn't recall. He shook his head in a quiet 'No.'

"We went to a Japanese restaurant by the beach, a nice little hole in the wall place. The waiter brought out a little Hibachi to our table and cooked chicken and shrimp skewers on it, right in front of us. You boys flipped, never having seen Hibachi cooking before."

Mike recalled the meal when she said it. Rose, gazing now at him, went on.

"There wasn't one thing I thought could have made the day any better than it was, until evening. You boys were bathed, in your pajamas and had been talking your dad's ear off about the beach. He was carrying on about how jealous he was we hadn't taken him too and he was making you both giggle about how you had forsaken him."

Mike was flooded with memories as Rose went on.

"I finished dinner dishes and sat on the sofa. Without a word, you both came over and sat on either side of me and said thank you for taking you to the beach. You both snuggled me and even hugged me without being asked. Matty was always the

169

snuggly one, but that night you were too, and at the same time! Well ... I just never had such a moment before."

Rose was beaming at Mike.

"I've had a wonderful life. I've dozens ... no, hundreds of such memories and I want to tell you a few more, because there's a point to this."

Rose told Mike stories about their family adventures and misadventures. She was recapitulating her life and it felt to Mike like she was saying thank you, or goodbye, to him somehow. It made him uneasy, in contrast to the joy that was in her eyes. She had more energy than was usual and she talked for over an hour. Toward the end Mike could feel her winding down and she became silent.

"Mike, I've had a long and lovely life, more than most get to have I think, and I'll be sad at not being here with you and Matty for more. I don't have another single regret and ... well, just one more ... I won't get to know my grandchildren in this life, but all in all, I can't complain."

Mike recognized her stab at humor at his expense and he smiled. She continued.

"I think you understand I'm dying and that it won't be long. That's why I've had you join me with Dr. Bedard and why I'm telling you all this."

170

Mike knew it, but he couldn't make himself say yes, and he sat in silence, looking at her. He felt large tears filling the wells of his eyes. They rolled down his expressionless face. He sat still and made no effort to wipe them away … he didn't care what it looked like.

Rose watched him, reached her hand to his face, and brushed the wet from his cheeks.

"It's ok sweet boy, I'm ready for this. It's a part of life and it's past my time."

Mike relaxed some at her touch and her powerful words, but his mind was reeling from the abruptness and depth of the emotion he felt. He tried but could think of nothing to say. He sat silently and waited for her to continue.

"I know this isn't fun to talk about, but honey, you must see how tired I am. I just don't have any fight left. I've felt this way for a long time, and I've something to ask of you. I have debated with myself for weeks if I even should be asking, but I need your help, and I think you'll see it's right for me. I want you to help me end this."

Mike had never been even close to being caught this far off guard. His speechlessness turned to numbness. His brain was there … he was self-aware, but he couldn't speak … he couldn't form a single thought.

Rose stopped talking and continued to hold his hand. She had a look he knew all too well. She would not speak again until he spoke. He rubbed the back of her hand affectionately and tears continued slowly rolling down his face, and he still could say nothing.

After a long pause, Mike began to have thoughts. He wasn't concerned with the religious aspects of suicide, or legalities, or the ethics of the request. He was realizing he was just incapable of having a part in her demise. It was unimaginable and he knew, deep in his heart, he could not do what she was asking.

"Mom, I admit I'm shocked and what I'm centering on are just two things. First, I understand why you want this, and I can't say you're wrong. My second thought is, as much as I'd want to give you whatever you may ever need or want, I know to my core I cannot do this for you. I'm so sorry Mom, but I can't."

Rose squeezed his hand again.

"It's ok, son. Truth be told, the second I heard it coming out of my mouth, I regretted saying it and knew it was a mistake to ask it of you. I want you to forget it and I apologize for bringing it up in the first place.

They kept to their own thoughts for a while and then Rose spoke again.

"Well, don't I feel a bit foolish now. I'll be fine son. Let's go home and you can help me get an appointment with one of those shrinks Dr. Bedard is trying to fix me up with. It's pretty clear I'm depressed and need one."

And that's what they did. They never spoke of it again and Rose made an appointment for a shrink. Mike put the incident out of his mind, and they went on, much as before, but never again did they make a trip to the mall.

Rose Jamison died six weeks and three days later.

Mike learned of it while at work. His watch commander had radioed for him to report to the station. The commander motioned Mike to a chair and with very little warning, but a fair amount of compassion, told him.

"Mike, I got a call from dispatch and an Anaheim P.D. officer was called to your mother's place. She has passed away in her sleep at home. I'm sorry to be the one to have to tell you."

Mike left work, still numb, after dressing out of his uniform, and arrived at Rose's apartment about 30 minutes later. The officer who had found her had been dispatched when one of

Rose's neighbors became worried that she wasn't answering her doorbell. Mike didn't know this officer, but he appreciated how low-key he was handling the scene.

The officer let Mike into the apartment to see her. Rose lay half reclined in her *spot* in the living room, the only way she could sleep at all, and she looked asleep. The television was on, as usual, and she looked … peaceful.

The officer told Mike her death appeared to have been of natural causes and he had spoken with her physician, Dr. Bedard. Her doctor concurred the death had been expected.

The officer told Mike the coroner, based on Dr. Bedard's statement, would not require an autopsy. Mike touched Rose's arm and he bent over, kissing her forehead one last time.

It would not occur to Mike until much later to wonder if she had committed suicide after all. Right then all he felt was a mixture of grief for himself and relief for her. He couldn't reconcile how he could feel both things at the same time, so he stopped thinking about his feelings and concerned himself with arrangements and notifying family and friends.

Days passed and Mike, grateful Matt had come home to be with them, slogged through the disposition of what remained of Rose's life. Rose had specified cremation and, a week later, with her memorials and her business done, Matt went home, and Mike went back to work.

Weeks had now passed, after those first hard days, and Christmas was near. Mike was home alone one morning when his doorbell rang. He answered, with no one was in sight, but UPS had dropped a package on his front step. Wondering if it was a Christmas gift or what, he carried the smallish package, wrapped in plain brown paper, inside and closed his door behind him. Mike couldn't tell where it was from by looking at the wrapper and he peeled the covering off. Inside was a dented, white, cardboard box with a large label.

It read *The Neptune Society* ... It was his mother's ashes.

What the hell! They sent my mother UPS ... in a crushed box?

He was furious for a moment, but then he had a picture pop into his head of his mom sitting on the couch in her *spot,* laughing her ass off and teasing him about the absurdity of it. He realized he was angry because he was embarrassed that he was starting to forget about her already, and thinking the package was a Christmas present from someone. It was true he had expected a call from The Neptune Society to come pick up her ashes, but it had been an assumption on his part.

Of course! Just box her up and ship her five-day ground! Why would they care?

He sighed and sat on his sofa with the box in his lap and he thought about her again. He placed her on the side table next to him, and in doing so, his eye was caught by his mom's volume of Shakespeare sitting next to it.

He had kept very few of her possessions … some plaster Christmas ornaments they had painted together, now the only decorations on his Christmas tree this year … her favorite coffee mug, which now served as a container for pens and markers on his desk … and the book.

He hadn't looked at the book since her death, but he wanted to look at it now.

He ran his hand across the smooth leather cover and went to open it. The pages fell open near the middle and he found a folded piece of writing paper tucked in the crease. He set the book down and unfolded the note. He would know his mother's penmanship anywhere and this was hers. On the paper she had handwritten a verse.

To be, or not to be? That is the question – Whether 'tis nobler in the mind to suffer the slings and arrows of outrageous fortune, or to take arms against a sea of troubles, And, by opposing, end them?"
Soliloquy from Hamlet – William Shakespeare

Mike recognized the verse as one of Shakespeare's most famous and he knew something about it that many people didn't. He knew Hamlet was talking about suicide.

What he didn't know was when, or why, his mom had copied it, or why she had left it here.

Could it just be a coincidence? She loved Shakespeare.

Or was this her very subtle way of letting him know she had opted out? Rose wouldn't have wanted anyone else to know, so she wouldn't leave a regular note spelling it out, or an upended bottle of pills laying around … nothing of the sort. She was way too smart for that. He tried to envision it. Pills? If she was going to do it, it would be pills.

So, what if she hadn't fought it, and opted out? What of it? A short and logical end to her pain and suffering, against a lifetime of joy and a hope of something better after life?

He just didn't know, but in his gut, the more he thought about it, he felt she hadn't done it, despite the copied verse. He decided she wouldn't want him to be in turmoil or unsure over it, so she most definitely would have left him a surer sign, if she was going to leave a sign for him in the first place, which he doubted. He thought it more likely she'd keep him in the dark, given his reaction when she had asked him to help her with it all those months ago.

He imagined what she would say if he asked her about it.

Does it matter son? Please think about my life when you think of me, and not my death ... think about how wonderful life was for me and how much I loved you and Matty.

The imagined conversation rang true to him.

He decided in the end he would never know for sure, and he chose to believe she fought until the end, because he asked her to.

And now ... they both could be at peace.

The Hospitallers

Hos.pi.tal.ler –

Noun: a member of a religious military order established in Jerusalem in the 12th century. (Webster's Dictionary)

"When Crusaders took Jerusalem in 1109, the master of the hospital was the monk, Gerard de Martignes. In 1113 he created a separate order of monks there, the Friars of the Hospital of St. John of Jerusalem. The objective of the order was to aid pilgrims to the Holy Land by operating several hospitals between Malta and Jerusalem. It soon became apparent military protection for the pilgrims was also necessary. This culminated in Gerard's successor, Raymond du Puy, reconstituting the order as both a military and medical order by integrating them with the Knights Templar."
(Encyclopedia.com)

James Boyd was present for the birth of the world-wide paramedic system, which occurred in Los Angeles County in the early 1970s.

He took pride in this, and it caused him to think back on how fortunate he had been to become one of the first paramedics of the modern age. He recognized he was being introspective because it was to be his last shift supervising the last trainee he would ever have, Ramón 'Ricky' Santiago. After nearly 30 years with the L.A. County Fire Department, James was retiring in just two more months.

It was just after 7 a.m. and as was usual for this time of day, the shift change at Fire Station #10 was in progress. As was also usual, there was a lot of animated joking going on and war stories being exchanged between the on-coming and off-going shifts. James' regular partner was Anthony Gibson, who was looking after Ricky.

Anthony and Ricky were both checking out their rescue rig and equipment, leaving him time to sip from a mug of their too-strong firehouse coffee. He was watching them from a short distance and had time to think while they went through their morning routine.

Anthony was giving Ricky good-natured grief about his incompetence and his embarrassingly slow progress in mastering this basic part of the job.

"Santiago, you may think this is your last shift as a trainee, but I don't know if I can live with passing your sorry ass and inflicting you on the public. I'll be doing a lot of soul-searching today."

Ricky kept working and replied,

"At least I know a stethoscope from a cotton swab, Sir."

"What? Are you talking crap to your training officer?"

Ricky looked at Anthony in mock surprise.

"No Sir! I said the stethoscope is fine, but we need more swabs, Sir! And I would never disrespect you, Sir."

"Santiago, it's going to take a lot more than ass-kissing to make you ready for this career. In order to function as a steely-eyed lifesaver, and part-time heartbreaker, one who is able to laugh in the face of danger, and snatch your fellow man from the jaws of death, you must consistently exhibit one thing I've yet to see from you … competence. You are nowhere near ready to kick death in the balls and take him to the mat."

James watched this exchange and felt some amount of pride in Ricky, whom he knew was going to be a fine paramedic. He thought about the differences in Ricky's introduction to this world and his own. Pouring himself another coffee, James continued watching his partner and trainee finish the well-worn routine of insuring they were ready to roll. He was watching, but he was more so thinking about the history of his profession right then.

Prior to paramedics emerging in the early 1970s as a profession, emergency medical responders in the U.S. had been mostly men untrained in even basic first aid. Across the country in those days, they drove ambulances owned and operated primarily by local mortuaries. James could recall as a boy in his own hometown there was a McCormick's Mortuary.

It was a stately Greek revival-style building on the main drag through the city. Parked in front of McCormick's, almost always, was a long, gleaming, white Cadillac ambulance under the front portico. The ambulance had fascinated him as a kid, and he remembered sneaking up to it and looking at the interior many times. It had a forest-green stripe painted down the length of each side and a huge red dome light and chrome siren on the roof. Inside the tight quarters of the back of the unit was a gurney with white sheets and straps and not much else.

In that era, a phone call from the city police department would dispatch the ambulance from the mortuary to the scene of gruesome accidents, or heart attacks, and the attendants would *swoop and scoop* the patients to the hospital, rendering little, if any first aid along the way. In the event the patient was dead at the scene, or died on the way, well, the boys knew where the mortuary was, didn't they?

James' musings were interrupted by the team moving on to the next part of the morning. Finished with razing the oncoming crew, the firefighters from the off-going shift had drifted off and gone home and James' team went about completing equipment and vehicle checks.

In addition to his two partners and himself, there was a fire engine staffed with a captain, an engineer, and two firefighters on his team.

The next part of the morning ritual was for them to all gather in the kitchen for the morning briefing with their captain, Eric Tanner. The crew would settle around the table in short order and Tanner would update them on everything pertinent to their world locally, then go on to outline what they would be doing during the day, be it drills, inspections, PR stops, or whatever.

Most of the crew made a habit of first taking a few minutes to stop by their spacious combined locker room and bath/shower room to spruce up and check their uniforms before briefing. While washing his face, James was approached by Ricky, who had a ridiculously earnest look on his face. Anthony, also present, heard Ricky when he spoke to James.

"Senior Training Officer Boyd, Sir, I regret I must inform you of mistreatment I have been subjected to by Firefighter Paramedic Anthony Gibson, Sir."

"Yeah? … What did he do, Ricky?"

"Sir, it's a little embarrassing but he … he … asked me for sexual favors Sir, implying I wouldn't pass probation if I didn't comply."

This brought choked-back laughter from the men present. It was restrained laughter because no one wanted to miss Boyd's response. Boyd grabbed a hand towel from his duffle and dried his face, then looked at Ricky earnestly.

"So, he asked you this as a favor?"

"Yes Sir, for all kinds of disgusting acts."

Boyd looked back to the mirror long enough to drag a brush through his hair a few times, then he tossed the brush into his bag. He hoisted the bag from the counter over his shoulder and looked back at Ricky.

"Well son, being it was asked as a favor, and was not an unlawful order, I'd recommend you decline his request."

Ricky was grinning and light snickering from the others in the room started to swell. James continued.

"As for myself – I'd thank you to never bring me a concern again which causes me to consider any aspect of your sex life. I have enough trouble sleeping as it is."

James walked casually off toward the adjacent bunkhouse to stow his bag, leaving a trail of laughter behind him, including, he could hear, Ricky's.

James was the first to settle in the kitchen for the morning briefing and, while waiting for the others, he gazed out the window and resumed thinking about the amazing history of his profession.

Where World War II and the Korean War had done much to advance emergency medicine in general, it took Vietnam to create the right conditions in the U.S. for paramedics to emerge. Over the course of that war, the military fielded about 5,000 combat medics. These men had gained serious skill sets in treating trauma victims, but they also were made surprisingly adept, by necessity, in treating a wide array of medical problems.

In the jungles and highlands of Asia, gunshot wounds and shrapnel didn't take nearly as many men out of action as more pedestrian medical ailments. Their troops suffered everything from trench foot to abscessed wisdom teeth and these men trusted the *Docs* knew what to do.

185

Over a dozen years, from the 60s, through the mid-70s, these new-age Hospitallers ... these warrior medics ... brought their skills home with them, providing the country with a large pool of trained and able talent and James had unwittingly become a part of it.

He had earned an associate degree in history at Santa Monica City College in 1970 and he was unsure what he wanted to do with his life. He was 19 years old and didn't have a clue where his life was going. He wondered if he should give up his college deferment for the draft and go into the service like so many of his friends had, or if he should keep going in school. Back then he wasn't afraid of going to war.

He didn't have nearly enough sense to be afraid at the time. Raised on John Wayne movies and saying the Pledge of Allegiance every morning in school, he was an American, a citizen of the greatest country in the world, he thought, and he worried more about being shamed later in life at not having served in the military than about being maimed or killed in war. He was typical of many in his generation.

On the other hand, there were many young people across the country involved in protests over America's involvement in the war. James was unconcerned with this, and he felt the protestors were misguided. He reasoned communism was a fatal and malignant political and social system. It had to be checked around the globe or it would eventually land on their country's doorstep.

As for peaceful resolution, his thought was any study of history makes clear non-violence and negotiation were useless in stopping governments, with their own myopic agendas, from imposing their collective wills on other governments and cultures. The violence of war, in fact, had solved more issues and conflicts in human history than all other means combined, in his opinion. To say violence never solved anything was simply wrong. It may not be pleasant or desirable, but it was a cold, hard, fact.

To help him decide what to do, James went to a military recruiting office. His idea was to check it out, *to kick the tires*, so to speak. He could at least decide which branch of the service suited him before making any final decisions.

The recruiting offices in town were situated separately, but next to each other, in an attractive and shaded strip mall. The Army had their office on the left, Air Force in the middle, and the Navy and Marines office was combined and on the right. James had parked in the lot to the right side of the complex, by chance, and he wandered into the Navy office first. It was a simple twist of fate which would guide the course of the rest of his life.

He remembered it as if it was last week. A fit-looking middle-aged Petty Officer greeted him as he entered the office. He was in uniform, but he conveyed warmth and put James at ease while guiding him to a comfortable chair.

"Petty Officer Gray - but call me Larry."

They talked about everything, except the military, for quite a while. Larry had explained he could best guide him in selecting a military job by learning about him as an individual. James could see why the Navy had seen fit to assign Petty Officer Gray to recruiting duty. He was a friendly and believable presence.

At a point in their talk Larry sat back.

"I've got it! I know the perfect job for you. It's as plain as day. You should be a Corpsman, you know, a medic."

James found he was attracted to this idea. Larry continued his patter without missing a beat.

"You would know, being a historian and all, there is a long tradition of warrior healers going all the way back to the Crusades. Well, carry the tradition into our times and you get the U.S. Navy Corpsman. And you have all kinds of options. You can be on ship, or attached to a Marine unit, or at a stateside clinic. It's a versatile specialty in the Navy. You might as well start learning the lingo. It's called an M.O.S., *Military Occupational Specialty*."

Within days, almost before he realized what was happening, James had enlisted and had orders to report for basic training in San Diego. He hadn't received as much grief from his parents as he had expected and having only a couple of casual girlfriends at the time, there wasn't much resistance there either.

So it was that he found himself, a few weeks later, on a bus to San Diego, excited and looking forward to the adventure of a lifetime.

He had no trouble during basic training and was proud of himself and excited when he was ordered to technical training for his rating as a 'Pharmacist Mate'. James still didn't know where he would end up in the Navy, but he applied himself and did well. It was then the surprise came.

At this point in the war, San Diego was a sprawling military complex, with subsidiary bases surrounding it, and following his 'Corpsman training' he was sent across the base to the Field Medical Service School at Camp Del Mar for eight weeks of Marine training.

189

It was here he learned the 'options' talked about by Petty Officer Gray were not options as much as remote possibilities and he and his classmates were all headed for only one place, assignment to Fleet Marines. This meant they were all in for assignment to Marine infantry units on the ground in Vietnam. They were here for a crash course in how to integrate themselves into Marine combat units.

There was hardly a more dangerous duty in the military to be found. For the first time since enlisting he felt unprepared for what was coming and as it turned out, he had no idea how right he was. After this last stateside school, there was one more school. James was put on a slow boat to Okinawa for jungle warfare training at Camp Schwab.

A few months later, upon graduating from Camp Schwab, James felt 100 percent unprepared for war, or for caring for wounded Marines. He had fired exactly one 30-round magazine of ammo through his M-14 rifle, fired two 15-round clips from his issued sidearm, and had three practice amphibious landings.

By the time they were finished with their courses in Okinawa, they were weary of schooling and resigned to shortly being sent into some kind of shit storm in Vietnam, which they might, or might not, survive.

James and his classmates were peeled off individually over the next few days for transport to their assigned Marine units in Vietnam. Most of them flew out on commercial airliners, which he found odd. His day came and he thought about the irony of eating peanuts and drinking cocktails, handed to him by a pretty stewardess, as he was being delivered to the front doorstep of mankind's most primitive occupation … war.

These flights of soldiers and sailors were routine and almost all of them were landing in Saigon or DaNang. Once *in Country*, they were sent without ceremony on a Jeep or Helicopter ride to be delivered to the units they had been assigned to.

James' recollections were yanked back to the present by his fellow medics, as they filed into the kitchen. He didn't feel like reliving any more of the war today anyway. Today was about what happened after *Nam*, and about how he lucked into the greatest job in the world and became Los Angeles County Paramedic number 142.

Captain Tanner ran through the daily briefing, describing local road closures in effect, departmental news, and a recap of the incidents responded to the previous day on *A* shift. The captain then outlined the plan for their day, which was a dry-hose drill at the elementary school.

Dry hose drills were favored by the team because it meant hundreds of feet of hose stretched out from the truck would not be filled with water after being run out. This meant half the work back at the station changing out the wet hose on the truck and reloading it with dry hose. It was a *dry-run* and it was most welcome.

Tanner continued.

"The reason for this ridiculously easy day has nothing to do with you all, who in fact still have richly-deserved punishment coming for shrink-wrapping my car closed last shift, but it has everything to do with Ricky Ricardo over here, who I am informed is dangerously close to finishing his field rotation without having killed anyone."

Snickering came from among the group.

"In fact, if he makes it through this shift, he can't be stopped. This must not be allowed to happen, so a short drill today and we stay available for every possible minute. Maybe we'll get lucky and catch a call where he kills someone in front of witnesses, and we can be done with his threat to the health and welfare of our citizenry."

The laughter was full-throated, and Ricky stood, bowing to the applause. Tanner wrapped up by poking a last bit of fun at James.

"Boyd, I'm disappointed. How'd a man of your experience let him get this far? All right everybody, let's saddle up and get this over with."

It was 8:05 a.m. when Engine 10 and Rescue 10 rolled out of the barn and went to drill.

On the way, Anthony and Ricky were talking about how the Dodgers' season was going and James, with only a mild interest in baseball, let his thoughts return to recalling the evolution of the paramedic program he had been a part of all these years.

He had returned from the war wiser and with a plan for his future. He was determined to take advantage of his veteran's education benefits and he enrolled at Cal State Fullerton. He was going to work for a degree in chemistry, a subject he had loved in high school and junior college, reasoning it would position him for a high paying job as a chemist.

As he neared finishing his degree program, finding a good job had become a priority. Quite by accident one day when he was scouring a job-board, he got wind the L.A. County Fire Department was hiring. He applied and after weeks and weeks of testing and interviews, he was excited when he landed a job as a firefighter recruit on the strength of his pending degree and military experience.

193

He sailed through the fire academy training and spent a short time as a rookie firefighter before being tapped for the new Los Angeles County paramedic program. L.A. County at the time had about a third of its stations staffed with paramedic teams and they were shooting for all their stations to be staffed by the end of the following year.

The force behind the program was a small cadre of doctors and politicians in state and county government who had launched the program just a few years before. The pilot program was successful, and this opened the door for what would turn out to be, in the years to come, a nearly worldwide shift in upgrading emergency care outside the hospital.

The designers of the program looked hard in the beginning to determine who these paramedics should be, and it became clear firefighters were a perfect for it. Ready to go 24 hours a day, bright and trainable, emergency responders already accustomed to working in teams. It was a lock. These boys were made to order.

The two initial teaching hospitals selected for the program were *L.A. Harbor Hospital* in San Pedro and *Daniel Freeman Hospital* in Inglewood. The two schools produced 150 Paramedics a year between them, plus or minus, and he had been one of the early ones.

It was 30 years on now and the first generation of paramedics were all but done passing on the torch. He was proud of his profession and of his place in it.

James' thoughts were interrupted yet again by the team's arrival at their drill site. The drills started and the day unfolded. After the drills, there were several opportunities for Ricky to kill someone during calls for service, but he didn't.

The shift flowed normally, and lunch came and went. They had been called out for a small kitchen fire where nobody had been hurt, two auto accidents with minor injuries, and shortly thereafter they responded to a call where a man was suffering a heart attack. Anthony and Ricky handled the calls flawlessly and the patient survived the trip to the emergency room. Another call came in for a young woman who had attempted suicide by deeply lacerating her wrists, and again James' protégécs performed flawlessly.

In the early evening, the team arrived back at the station, and it was Anthony and James' turn to make dinner for the crew. They rustled up a huge garden salad and baked chicken with rice pilaf for everyone. Afterward, Anthony brought out a cake for dessert. It was made by his wife and looked like the character from the game "Operation" in honor of Ricky's passing the program.

With dinner done, the crew retired to the *day room* for television and Ricky was doing dishes. James had a habit for coffee and drank it morning, noon, and night. He poured a cup and sat in the kitchen while Ricky filled the sink with suds.

"Well, it looks as if you made it Ricky. What do you think?"

Ricky paused for a moment.

"I'm sure it won't surprise you, but I feel great. I'm excited and happy, and just a little bit scared."

James nodded and took a sip of coffee.

"That's normal enough, for sure. It's a big responsibility and truthfully, an honor to be entrusted with the lives of others. I've been thinking of any last-minute advice I could share with you, which would stick with you for a career. I've been thinking on it all day, actually."

Ricky finished the dishes and looked at James while drying his hands. He poured a cup of coffee for himself and sat at the table with James.

James continued.

"All kidding aside, I've got this idea I want to cap your training with a history lesson. I want to put this vocation into a historical context for you. I want you to remember you're not a

movie star, but a healer. You serve the sick and injured …
you're a Hospitaller. "

Ricky's eyes widened at James' unusual line of thought.
James talked to him for over an hour about the history of
emergency medicine, Hospitallers, war-time medics, and a few
of his own experiences. It was clear Ricky was enthralled with
his accounts and James felt good. He'd done his best and the
boy was good.

"Well, we will get through whatever comes our way
tonight, then you are off to your first assignment."

Ricky, in uncharacteristic fashion, formally thanked
James for his mentorship.

"Seriously boss … you made it easy for me and I really
want to thank you for guiding me through my field training. I
learned a lot from you. Thank you."

They shared the moment and then joined the group in the
day room.

Later in the evening, the crew was sent out to cover a
traffic accident and it was a bloody mess. Three vehicles were
involved at high speeds. It had taken James a few years, but he
learned to step back let his trainees work, only stepping in when
they were about to seriously screw up.

He watched Ricky and Anthony work as a team, walking to each patient and triaging them, requesting more ambulances, getting the engine crew directed on patient extraction and first-aid efforts.

It was going smoothly when Ricky focused on a woman pinned into the driver side of an ancient faded blue Ford Taurus. She was conscious, but barely, and it was clear she had internal injuries. As Ricky was leaning in near the smashed-out driver's window of her car, James watched and listened as Ricky brushed blood-matted locks from her eyes and told her what was going on, calming her, explaining all they were doing to get her out.

And then it happened ... the magic moment when James knew with certainty, he could retire in peace.

The battery in the demolished Taurus began arcing. Sparks were flying from underneath the crushed hood and the ground below was soaked with leaking gasoline ... enough to send any sane person running the other way. James watched as Ricky instinctively nearly leaped into the car, placing himself between the ignition source and his patient, protecting her.

One of the crew doused the engine block with a CO_2 extinguisher, while another ripped out the battery cable.

James breathed a sigh of relief when the situation was again under control, and he felt a swelling of pride in his heart for Ricky. James had just witnessed the birth of a Hospitaller. He knew one when he saw one, and he knew he could leave *The Order* in peace now; he knew it was in good hands.

The Interview

The academic advising offices for Cal State Fullerton filled the majority of the first floor of the admin building. On a gorgeous California morning an attractive woman, walking while balancing an oversized shoulder bag and a large Starbucks, approached the entrance. Corrine Biondi was on the University staff, a student advisor for the past 12 years, and you wouldn't know it to look at her, but she led a double life. She was also a paid *consultant* for the Central Intelligence Agency of the U.S. government.

Her husband sometimes teased her that she was a *Spy*, but she wasn't. In her case, it simply meant she was a talent scout for the agency, identifying students with specific and promising skills and records and forwarding this information to a designated agency recruiter. Corrine knew there was at least one of *her* on almost every college campus in the United States. Even though she was paid, the truth was, being very patriotic, she would have done the extra work for free.

She set her bag on the side table by her desk and enjoyed a last swig of her still-warm latte before sitting at her desk.

Well, let's see who we have this morning. David Atwater at 9:45, and then Monica Hiyashi at 10:30. So, I've time to take a walk-in student now, and another at 11:15.

She opened a file drawer and fingered through a short stack of special files,

Atwater, and ... Hiyashi.

Pulling the two files out, she set them on the desk and opened the top one.

Alright Mr. Atwater let's refresh on your situation. Yes, I remember ... a Spanish speaker ... History major, Junior, 3.8 GPA, four years in the Army as an infantryman, but no travel or experience outside the U.S. ... hmm ... A very gringo name for a Spanish speaker. Where'd he learn it? ... Oh, yes, his mother, Venezuelan.

Corrine flipped through a few more pages.

Notes from my last chat with Jim Duncan

'Agency soft check green, guide David to Latin American Studies, encourage semester abroad in Mexico/South America'

Okay Mr. Atwater, we'll see if you're the adventurous sort or not this morning.

She opened the other file on her desk, studied it, then set them both aside.

Okay, I'm ready, Let's grab a walk-in.

A bit later in the morning, David Atwater strolled across the campus yard, going from his history class to his appointment with Mrs. Biondi. He had fifteen minutes to get there and was unhurried. The class he was coming from, *History 453 – Mexico, pre-Columbian to the missionaries*, was on his mind.

Cortez ... what a tool he was! Ruthless bastard. Unbridled power ... and greed.

The lecture that morning detailed how Cortez had taken 600 conquistadors, leaving from the port of Vera Cruz, and he gathered additional warriors along the way from those natives who were already hostile toward the Aztecs. Cortez used them all to conquer an entire civilization.

All for gold ... Professor Reyes is right about one thing, Cortez beat unbelievable odds, driven by pure ambition.

David's thoughts were interrupted when he saw an extraordinarily attractive co-ed walking his way. As they neared each other their eyes met, and both smiled. Neither spoke as they passed, but she hadn't broken eye contact with him. He sighed as he walked on.

Jeez, she is smokin'! ... It's not like I didn't have a minute to chat her up. When am I going to get back into the pool? ... not yet.

David's high school girlfriend had dumped him while he was in the Army and though he'd been back for almost two years already, he'd been too busy with a full-time job and full-time school, to focus on romance. On top of that, he was somewhat shy for such a handsome lad.

Time enough for that will be coming when I graduate.

David saw the admin building up ahead and angled for it. Once inside, he signed in and waited in the lobby. Corrine appeared a few minutes later and ushered him into her office. They exchanged pleasantries on the way and David was guided to a comfortable chair near her desk. She got straight to the point.

"David, I see you're a history major and you now have five semesters of straight A's in Spanish so far. Are you fluent?

David flushed slightly.

"The truth is my mom has only spoken to me in Spanish my whole life. She speaks English to everyone else, but she's an absolute nut job about me being bilingual. She says it will be my most valuable life skill someday. I took Spanish all through high school and now here, mostly because … well, they're easy credits for me."

Corrine nodded.

"Esta Bien! A wise woman, your mother. She's right of course. Now, as far as social sciences go, there are two traditional venues for career focus. There is teaching, at all levels, and there is government service, the departments of State, Defense, and the CIA. Looking over your transcripts, as a junior you are actually well positioned to go in any of these directions."

David became a history major when he first enrolled because he wasn't sure of what he wanted to do in life and because in high school History was his favorite subject. It seemed at the time a good place to start and nothing since had grabbed his interest more.

He'd already rejected teaching as a career, thinking it would be too routine for him, but he hadn't yet considered government service. The possibilities bloomed in his mind.

"If I wanted to pursue government service, what would that look like?"

Corrine scanned his transcripts for a moment and couldn't help but think her job was going to be too easy today.

"If you go the government service route, with your language skills, you are best served by changing your major to a geographically focused degree within the social sciences. It could be Asian studies, or Mid-East studies, but given you are already adept with the Spanish language, Latin American studies is for you. It'll change your future course selections very little, and you'll have no ground to make up in meeting graduation credits for the new major."

Mrs. Biondi sensed David was biting and gave a sharp yank on the hook.

"The good news is you don't have to decide right now, and your timing is right to take advantage of the perfect vehicle for making an informed decision. There's about two weeks left to sign up for a semester abroad in Mexico or Central America. Are you familiar with the program?"

David had heard about the program and Corrine quickly filled in the blanks. He hadn't considered it before. His biggest disappointment with his Army experience was when he hadn't gotten to *see the world*, as his recruiter had promised him. Corrine dug a few brochures out of her top drawer and slid them across the desk.

"Look at these for a minute and I'll answer any questions you may have."

She busied herself with notations in his file while David read and thought.

I'd have to quit my job, but so what? I have VA benefits and I've been banking Grandma's inheritance money, ten grand, and two years of paychecks. I can afford it, and no one is keeping me here. How awesome would it be to go and bum around Central America for a few months!

After gleaning all the particulars from the brochures, David was half-ready to leave for Mexico the next day. The opportunity was creating a growing excitement in him. Corrine then made the point which knocked him over the edge.

"The very best part of this program is it is a clear resumé builder, meaning when you go to get work in your field, the time spent in this program will be viewed as actual and practical work experience, something the majority of your competitors for jobs won't have."

And like that, it was done. David decided he was going. They wrapped up their meeting and David, preparations checklist in hand, thanked her and left.

Corrine smiled to herself and closed David's file. She was ready for her next student.

About a week after he set his plans in motion, David was on campus in the student union studying between finals. Christmas was near and he was feeling good about everything. He was set to go. He had coordinated his arrangements to depart for Guatemala the second week of January and to return in the last week of August. Six months of adventure were a month away and he couldn't wait.

His mother was nearly as excited as he was, which surprised him some, but she explained it was important to her that he experience the other half of his roots. She said she was also excited for him because it would be an amazing adventure for him.

David's pleasant self-distraction from studying was interrupted by a man speaking to him.

"David Atwater! … Hello."

David looked up, unsure if he was the one who was being addressed.

"Um, hello."

A middle-aged, fit-looking man, with short graying hair smiled and stepped up to him with his hand extended.

"I didn't mean to startle you. I know we haven't met. I'm Jim Duncan. Your guidance counselor, Mrs. Biondi, mentioned to me you might be interested in serving your government."

David's eyebrows lifted as he shook the offered hand.

"Yes, we talked about it a short while back … umm, what … where in government are we talking about?"

Duncan smiled.

Well son, I'm recruiting for the CIA. I thought we could get together, have a cup of coffee after your class, and compare notes, see if there might be a fit here somewhere."

David could have been knocked over by a feather, but he recovered quickly.

"Yeah, I wasn't expecting … I didn't know you guys … Yes, I'd be interested in talking with you, Mr. Duncan."

Duncan chuckled.

"I understand. We are a bit direct sometimes in our approaches with candidates. You're out of classes at two o'clock today, yes? Can you meet me on the other side of Highway 57 over there at Coco's Restaurant at two-thirty?"

David was surprised at first, but then it was clear his school schedule was furnished to Duncan by Mrs. Biondi.

"I was going to ask you how you know my school schedule, but that would be dense of me, wouldn't it?"

Duncan gave a full laugh.

"Indeed, but there's nothing sinister afoot, I promise. It's just a meet and greet. You might call it a *pre-interview*. More for you to consider us than vice versa."

Duncan smiled at David and offered his hand again.

"It was a pleasure meeting you son. See you at two-thirty across the way."

David shook his hand again and Duncan casually walked off, disappearing into the quad.

After class, David went straight to the restaurant and found Duncan already sitting in a booth. David scooted himself into the booth across from Duncan and greeted him. Their waitress appeared and David declined ordering any food but said yes to coffee. Duncan was relaxed and friendly and started off their conversation.

"I bumped into Connie, Mrs. Biondi, this morning and she mentioned that you're changing your major and she told me about your pending trip to Guatemala. My thought was it's a good time for me to introduce myself and talk with you about a career as a case officer if you had any interest in hearing about it."

David was interested but wasn't sure yet what he wanted to ask. Duncan filled in with a question for him.

"How'd you come to choose Guatemala as your destination, David?"

"At first, I was thinking about Mexico, but I found a travel guide that talked about all the mom-and-pop Spanish schools in Antigua, just up the mountain from Guatemala City. I figure I can get a little polish on my Spanish, but mostly it's because Guatemala is at the center of the region. I plan on using Antigua as a hub, bouncing back and forth between there and all the places I want to see."

Duncan smiled and nodded.

"An excellent choice! They've got a bunch of private schools with one-on-one instruction for what pencils out to about two dollars an hour, and you can travel to all the other countries there in one day or less. It's a priceless experience really."

David appreciated the thought. He had a few questions for Duncan now and changed the subject.

"What can you tell me in general about the CIA? I'm not even sure what to ask."

Duncan didn't miss a beat.

"Here's the unvarnished truth of it. Foreign service is an amazing career, but it's not for everyone. In the case of *The Agency,* it's for even fewer. The life of a case officer can be extremely distasteful and sometimes dangerous. It's a very nasty and unforgiving occupation. To survive and thrive you must bring deep and refined understandings of history, politics, ethics, civics, psychology, sociology, and philosophy to the table. It's how you'll weather the storms of your career."

Duncan stirred his coffee, then continued.

"The hardest part, in my opinion, is wrapping your head around the justification for using people, putting them in harm's way, and possibly leading them to their deaths, to develop spies to betray their country, and to, at need, abandon them and sometimes their families, to torture and death … It is bitter. Some assets you end up liking, and some you don't. Spies are motivated by many things and it's a subtle skill to find and turn people against their own government. I guess I'd say that unless you can truly believe in the greater good of protecting American interests and of the promotion of freedom for people everywhere, it's a bridge too far."

David thought he understood.

"What about personal danger and risk?"

Duncan answered directly.

"I won't say it's not there, it is, but it's not like you might imagine from the movies. It depends a lot on where you're posted and who your people are spying on. You'll do little, if any, direct spying yourself. You technically won't be a spy; you'll be a spy manager."

David was processing what he'd been told and didn't speak. Duncan continued.

"It's an awful lot to take in and think about, but we believe it's very important to be up front and realistic with candidates. Let me leave you with two tasks to complete before you get back to the states, which will help you know if it's for you. Task one: I want you to go out and buy three books and take them with you ... knowledge is power. You will think I'm nuts because never in your life will you again read three more dissimilar volumes. Got a pen?"

David looked at Duncan quizzically and dug a note pad and pen from his bookbag. Duncan continued.

"Book one, *The Arco CIA Entrance Examination Study Guide.* It offers a surprisingly good overview of what the career requirements and challenges are. Book two, *The Good Spy, the Life and Death of Robert Ames.* It's by a guy name of Kai Bird and is probably the best snapshot out there of what the life is like. Book three, *Starship Troopers* by Robert Heinlein. Here is where you will become certain I'm a loon. It's a silly Sci-Fi yarn, but it's hiding one of the best philosophical essays on social responsibility, civics, warfare, and aspiring to the greater good, that's ever been written, in my opinion."

David noted the list, and Duncan rounded out his thoughts.

"Task two – when you've been in Guatemala for four months or so, call the U.S. Embassy in Guatemala City and ask for the public relations officer. Identify yourself to him or her and explain you are a student abroad and would like to interview a career foreign service officer for a paper you need to write for school. They will contact you later with an appointment. Go and interview the person they set you up with. That's it. Do these things and you will know if you want to make the leap."

David was more intrigued than ever, and his intentions were to execute both tasks.

Duncan pulled his wallet out and threw down a ten on their check.

"Come see Mrs. Biondi right away when you get back and I'll find you for another chat. In the meantime, all three of those books are in stock at the Barnes and Noble by your mom's place. I checked."

Duncan slid out of the booth, shook David's hand, and smiled.

"Take care and enjoy your adventure."

And he was gone.

A month later, David, exams completed and with the holiday's past, arrived in the evening hours at Los Angeles International Airport for his flight. Delta Airlines flight 1545 left

L.A. at 1:45 a.m., and five hours later was on a soft descent into the heart of Guatemala. The passengers were beginning to stir in preparation for landing.

David reached to his chest, out of nervousness, and touched the travel pouch hung around his neck. The feel of his passport and cash pouch under his shirt made him feel more secure, and he looked out of his tiny window. The rays of the rising sun cut between glowing clouds. He saw a range of volcanic mountains and how the morning light flooded the sprawling basin of Guatemala City below, bathing it in a beautiful orange hue. They landed.

His entry to the country through customs was easy. He answered a few questions to explain the purpose of his visit, then was thrilled when the agent picked up a big rubber stamp and authoritatively pounded a page on David's passport, leaving a gorgeous entry stamp. The agent efficiently closed it and handed it back to David.

"Welcome to Guatemala Señor. Enjoy your stay."

Confident now, David exited the airport and was met by a blast of humidity and colorful noises and smells such as he had never experienced. Airports are airports, but this was different. Hundreds of people, all in urgent motion, were talking, whistling, moving in and out of each other's paths. Dilapidated

215

buses belching noisy plumes of blue smoke, motorcycles with two riders zipping dangerously between a sea of honking taxis – it was controlled chaos.

David must have looked lost as a woman approached and stood before him, and just looked at him. Surprising to David, she spoke to him in English. After determining he was bound for Antigua, she bid him to follow her with a nod, not looking back to see if he had.

He did, and soon caught up with her. They walked in silence, navigating between other travelers for two or three minutes before arriving at a curb where a bus was parked.

"This is for you. You have exchanged dollars for quetzals already?"

He pulled a ready wad of quetzals of various denominations from his front pocket and fanned them before her. She pointed to a 10-quetzal note.

"Give this one, you will get change."

David thanked her. She smiled, looking him in the eye.

"De nada."

Before she moved to leave, he peeled off another 10-quetzal note and handed it to her, but she politely refused.

"No, thank you. My wish is for foreigners to see the beauty of our country and the people. I am only doing my part. Welcome to Guatemala."

She smiled again and walked away into the crowd.

David looked after her for a moment and then turned to look at the bus. It was a converted school bus, painted primarily blue, but with an amazing array of other bright colors and pattern details. David looked at the destination placard above the front windshield, which read *Esmeralda*.

David was confused for a moment, then understood. The destination placards on all the buses he could see were girls' names. He guessed correctly the buses were independently owned and named and painted by the owners to distinguish them from their competitors.

The bus was filling up with travelers and commuters of all types; workers in regular clothes, Mayan Indians in traditional garb, farmers in sackcloth shirts and pants carrying baskets, and so on. People were talking softly amongst themselves, and a sappy ballad could be heard coming from the driver's radio on the dashboard. Soon the seats were filled, and they were off.

The city was a puzzle with a vibrant commerce but mixed with scenes of poverty-stricken people openly picking through rubbish heaps for food and dozens of hopeless alcoholics sprawled on public walkways in the mid-morning light.

Such an amazing contrast of rich and poor.

Esmarelda climbed out of the city and after about an hour of winding upward over mountain roads, they were rolling past mountainous jungles with volcanic peaks in the distance. Then suddenly, they crested a hill and the city of Antigua lay below.

David got off the bus when it stopped at the central market and walked the few cobble-stoned blocks to the Inn where he had arranged for his room by the week. Antigua was somehow calmer than the Capital. It was distinctively old … Spanish Colonial.

All the homes were whitewashed pastels with heavy wooden doors and high windows and high walls. But when the front doors were opened by residents coming and going, he could see lush open courtyards, covered walkways, and fountains inside. They were miniature Shangri La's. He was overwhelmed by the time he reached his Inn. Once in his room, he dropped his backpack, fell into his bed, and took a long afternoon nap.

The rest of David's first week in Guatemala was more interesting and exciting than he could have imagined. Different sights, smells, sounds, and tastes washing over him all day long, every day. There were firecrackers going off all over the city to scare away evil spirits, and he became accustomed to unfamiliar and colorful birds being a frequent sight.

Antigua was almost *alien* to him. He experienced daily thunderstorms in the warm afternoon air, saw uniformed soldiers with machine guns guarding banks, and he was frequently treated to street musicians. There was always a light and pleasant smell of wood-smoke in the air everywhere he went, and he marveled at how genuinely friendly almost everyone was.

One afternoon he clapped with other pedestrians when, out of nowhere it seemed, a small parade of a brass band and six 10-foot-tall *saints* danced by them on the street. The *saints* were men walking inside of narrow wood-pole frames draped in yards of colorful silks and cottons. The head of each figure was carved from wood and intricately painted in the likeness of various deities.

The thought of these *saints* and how they appeared to have been absorbed into the day-to-day local culture caused

David to think about how Catholicism itself had collided with Mayan polytheism.

He wondered if it were true that, over centuries, the two faiths had morphed into a blending of Mayan deities with saints and the Trinity. David supposed that the Mayans had, early on, suborned their gods to the priests herding them into church every seventh day (Probably at gunpoint in the beginning).

Choc - the god of rain - was transferred to the personage of Saint Martin, and *Ah Puch* - the god of destruction – was morphed into Lucifer.

Ixchel - the goddess of fertility - was a perfect stand-in for the Virgin Mary, and of course *Quetzalcoatl* - the god of learning and crafts - was none other than Jesus.

David was intrigued with these thoughts because he had been looking for topics to write on for his required semester-abroad papers. He was inspired now, by chance, to research and write on this insight to see how true or untrue his guesses were.

The *saints* passed him, twirling and dancing in time with the music, their hollow arms swinging widely and in time with the twisting rhythm of the hidden men underneath the frames as they passed down the street. David felt there was no end to the enchantment he could feel in Antigua.

After the impromptu parade, David walked to his chosen Spanish language school, the *Centro Linguistico Antigua,* paid his first week, and settled in with his individual teacher, a pleasant 20-something girl named Antonia. He had arranged for two hours a day of language instruction and he couldn't have asked for a nicer setting.

The *school* was a private home, set up with a dozen small tables around a central outdoor courtyard with fountains, potted flowering plants, and a few perched parrots populating the space. It was perfect.

David walked the city for hours after class each day and felt like he knew his way around well. He toured the museums in town and spent one afternoon at the Mayan cultural center, listening to folk music. He went into churches and markets and shops and soaked himself in the culture. Antigua was a city of mystery to him, and he found himself wondering at times what mind-blowing experience would present itself next.

Amid these experiences though, he hadn't forgotten Jim Duncan's advice and he had managed to read the books by the end of his fourth month in Antigua. He wasn't exactly bored by then, but he was keen for something new.

To his amazement, his Spanish was so highly polished by now that he found himself regularly thinking and dreaming in

221

Spanish. He had taken several two to four-day excursions from Antigua to Chichicastenango, Tikal, Copán, Lake Atitlan, and he'd been back to Guatemala City a couple times for plays and museums. Now he was feeling like he needed a vacation from his vacation. He needed a purpose. He started thinking a lot about his talks with Mrs. Biondi and Jim Duncan and he was inching in on a decision about what to do with his life. Duncan had been right, the books were so different, but all cast light onto what was involved in being an intelligence officer and he was increasingly attracted to the idea.

I'll call the embassy today and set up my interview with a foreign service officer.

And he did. He was surprised when he was placed on a short hold and a woman came back on.

"Hi, this is Katrina Espinosa. I'm the cultural attaché here. Is this David?"

Hi, yes, I'm David."

"Great! Jim Duncan told me to expect your call a while back. Listen, I've been itching for an excuse to get up to Antigua anyway, how about I come up Friday afternoon and we can do your interview and that'll leave me free to start my weekend early?"

"Sure, yeah, it saves me a trip too."

"Perfect, there's a restaurant inside the Ramada Hotel there. I'll meet you at 2 o'clock on Friday. I'll be wearing a blue scarf."

David was forming a response, but he was too slow. The line went dead.

Wow! That was easy. I guess I should get busy and outline my interview questions.

Friday came and David showed at the Ramada. He was familiar with the hotel because even though he wasn't staying there, he had bought day passes at the pool there several times to swim and drink Sangrias. He had wondered if this *Ramada Hotel* was affiliated with the Ramada Inn chain he knew of from the states, but he hadn't cared enough to research the question. He found Katrina easily and joined her at her table.

"Oh my, David, but you're a handsome one! I'm Katrina Espinosa, but you can call me Kat."

She met his gaze and held it with a smile, then shook his hand lightly. David couldn't help himself and he knew he was blushing.

"Hi Kat, thanks for meeting me up here."

"Listen, like I said, you're doing me the favor. I've got your lunch today. What will you have?"

223

They talked and ordered, and talked some more, and David was soon at ease with her. He found himself talking about his life much more than was usual for him, but he trusted her. With their lunch finished, David set to asking his *interview* questions.

It took David a minute to catch on, but then he noticed that for each question he asked, she asked one of him in return while he was jotting down her responses. She seemed very interested in what David thought of the books Jim Duncan had recommended to him. David stared at her.

"Wait a minute … You're CIA, aren't you?"

She beamed back at him; her eyes locked onto his.

"A smart one too!"

David thought about it.

"Of course, I should have guessed it sooner."

David was stuck for what to say. Kat's smile softened.

"You're quicker than most. That's good, but don't worry, there's nothing sinister here. We're just checking in to see what you think."

"Man, you guys use that line a lot."

"What?"

"Never mind, let me ask you something off the wall … Is it worth it? Is it worth what you have to give up?"

Kat tilted her head and sat back, paused in thought, as if she had made a quick decision.

"It depends on the person, but one thing is sure, you must be strong of mind and will. You have to think of yourself as a warrior, because it's what we really are underneath it all."

It rang true in David's ear.

"What's next if I want in?"

Kat's Cheshire grin returned, and she responded playfully.

"Why, you go back to Fullerton and finish college, dummy!"

They laughed quietly.

"One step at a time David. They'll bring you along in steps. I have a next step for you in mind, if you're game to put your toe in the water."

"I'm game."

"Okay, you know this job is mostly about developing assets. I want you to jump in the pool and try out your water wings now. If you'll look casually to your right, you'll see a table with three women, one of them wearing a pink shirt and jeans."

Kat kept her gaze on him as he casually glanced to his right. He saw the woman. She was attractive, about 25 or so, and she seemed to be having a good time. David looked back to Kat, and she continued.

"Have you ever seen her before? Do you know who she is?"

He shook his head no.

"Her name is Ariana Costanza. She is the step-daughter of Daniel Ortega ... *the* Daniel Ortega, The President of Nicaragua."

David was stunned. He took a moment to form a question.

"You're not joking. It's no accident we're having lunch here right now, is it?"

Kat grinned slightly.

"Not a chance bright boy. This is nowhere near an official CIA operation, but ... it's a juicy opportunity, not to be wasted. When we finish up lunch, if you're still game, go to your room and grab some clothes for two days. She's staying here this weekend. We've booked you into room 116. You'll be on your own in this. We can't offer any support or resources and you won't even know we're around, but we will be. More than anything David, this is a test-drive to help you to decide if this *pirate's life* is for you, or not. Instructive for you and certainly entertaining for us."

Kat was beaming at him. David decided to stop acting like an innocent tourist and take it all at face value.

"Okay, I'm in … Check into room 116, then what? I need intel … lots of it, what do you have? And what is it I'm after?"

Kat seemed pleased and smiled.

"Most excellent questions! You're a natural. We'd like to know why she's in Guatemala, number one, and two, does she have any dirt on daddy that we can use? There have been reports of tension between them. Cozy up to her, befriend her, get her talking, and preferably, drinking. Take her to bed if you can … do what presents itself. If she passes out, rifle her room; if she doesn't, give her those Clark Kent eyes of yours and get her to bare her soul to you. Are you following me?"

David was into it. He nodded and made his decision.

"Alright. Thanks for lunch. I'll be back in an hour."

David felt like a live wire walking back to his room, but he refused to indulge in disbelief. He knew damn well what he was doing, and why. It excited him. He was at the Ramada in less than an hour. He checked in and decided to get to work immediately. He needed a plan.

He reasoned if Ariana was going to stick around the hotel, she'd be out by the pool. If not, he'd have to follow her into town and find an excuse to talk with her there. There was still some daylight, so his best guess was the pool. He pulled on his trunks and shades, then headed poolside. Strike one. He waited for over an hour and she didn't show.

Damn! What now? Get dressed, check the bar, and if she's not there, head into town and see if you can run into her shopping.

David didn't find her in the bar, and he went into town. After three hours of looking, he still hadn't seen Ariana. Strike two. Returning to the hotel, he found the perfect spot to watch from in the bar. He had views into the restaurant and the lobby, enough where he could see almost everyone coming and going from the hotel.

He felt awkward in a way, trying to act like a spy, but he wanted to really see if he had a knack for it. He knew it was important for him to blend in and not call attention to himself, but he shouldn't actually drink. When he was sure no one was looking, he poured his beer into a very large potted plant within arm's reach of his table and when the waiter came by a few minutes later, he ordered another.

This is ridiculous! What am I doing here? ... Don't be a crybaby, you know what you're doing, and you're doing it as best you can. This opportunity is for you, make it count!

After about 45 minutes David saw Ariana and another girl walk into the hotel together, carrying shopping bags. They had been in town after all, and he'd missed them. The girls bustled past the bar, talking, and laughing, as they headed towards a hallway of guest rooms.

Okay! Wait or follow? ... Damn! ... Follow, get her room number, play it off like you're headed for your own room.

David was about to stand but stopped short. He saw a muscular middle-aged man in a suit following the girls. David guessed rightly the man was a bodyguard for Ariana.

Plan B, you can't tangle with a bodyguard if he gets suspicious of you. Wait for her to come out; you know where she is now.

David played his part of the lonely tourist while he waited. He nursed his beer and again poured it into the planter. He ordered another when a waitress came around and killed some time writing in his journal and then two postcards home. The girls emerged from the hallway and David saw them head straight for the restaurant off the lobby.

He casually got up and fell in behind them. By the time David reached the host's podium, the girls were seated at a table and their bodyguard was discreetly standing off to the edge of the dining room, about 15 feet from them. David asked for a window seat, which happened to be the table next to the girls. He was in position to engage with Ariana, and he had no idea what to say to her.

Come on Atwater, come up with something charming ... Nothing? ... damn it!

David affected looking at his menu and thought about his best approach.

Slow down, don't rush this. Listen to them, something will present itself.

The girls were talking about their purchases, then they started talking about where they wanted to go later for drinks and dancing. David hated dancing, but he knew he'd do it in a heartbeat tonight if needed, and he'd act like he was loving it.

"Excuse me ladies, I couldn't help overhearing you talking about nightclubs. I'm not from here and am looking for a club with good music and dancing. Do you know of any?"

The girls stopped talking and looked at him. Neither smiled nor answered.

Well ... they're having none of it.

"Sorry, I guess that sounds like crap to you, but it's true. I'm traveling alone and am just looking for somewhere fun to go. I didn't mean to bother you."

David looked away from the girls and pretended to be reading his menu again. He saw movement in the corner of his eye and looked around to see the bodyguard approaching him in what felt like a threatening manner. Ariana saw it too and stopped the man, putting up a hand.

"Sebastian, it's okay. The gentleman is from a different culture and allowances must be made."

The bodyguard, Sebastian, accepted this without comment and returned to where he had been watching from. David returned his gaze to Ariana.

"Wow … I was boorish and oblivious at the same time. You're a person of some importance it seems. Again, my apologies."

This must have warmed Ariana enough to forgive him.

"You are from the U.S., yes? I can tell from your clothes, but not your accent. Your Spanish is very good."

David ran with the opening.

"My mother is Venezuelan, she taught me. I'm David. May I at least know your names before I leave here in shame?"

David did have a certain charm when he chose to apply it and this comment got a giggle out of both girls.

"I'm Ariana."

"I'm Cassandra."

David nodded to them in turn.

"Well, it's nice to meet you both. I apologize again for making you uncomfortable."

Ariana looked at him frankly.

"It's fine, think nothing of it. Good evening, sir."

Ariana looked away and resumed talking with Cassandra in lower tones.

What just happened? She shut me down. Did I say something else wrong? No, she just dismissed you. I suck at this!

David, feeling disappointed in himself, endured his meal and left the restaurant as soon as appearances permitted, without speaking with the girls again. He glanced at Ariana as he rose to leave and gave her a cursory smile. She smiled in return but said nothing.

David walked out and headed for his room.

David Atwater, master spy and seducer. What was I thinking? That wasn't even fun. I can't follow them out tonight, it will look contrived ... All I can think to do is hang by the pool tomorrow and hope they come out.

David was mentally exhausted. He went to bed and had a dreamless sleep. The next day, he stuck to the hotel and to the pool area for most of the day but didn't see Ariana. He went into town later looking for her, but again did not see her. By the afternoon he had enough.

I don't think I've any talent for spy work. After this performance, I don't think I could get an interview with the CIA for a Janitor's position.

David never saw Ariana again and for all he knew she had checked out and left. He was a miserable spy. He entered his room at the Ramada in the late afternoon and sat on the edge of the bed. He saw a folded note left on his nightstand and read it.

D -

Breakfast - Doña Louisa's

8 a.m.

K -

"A woman of few words. Okay Kat, I'll be there."

He had dinner in the hotel and then went to bed.

When he woke the next morning, David felt good. He checked out of the hotel and trekked back to his rented room. After dropping his gear, he noted it was almost time to leave to meet with Kat. Having nothing else to do, he left early and was back on the street. As he made his way to Doña Luisa's, he thought about the past few days and how outlandish they had been.

He felt like he was not good at espionage and what was more, he didn't think he would enjoy the lifestyle. It was almost a relief. He would meet with Kat, but afterward he'd be looking forward to forgetting about the CIA and enjoying the remaining weeks of his trip.

His musings were interrupted as he approached the town's central park. He couldn't help himself and he had a few minutes to spare, so he grabbed a seat on an open bench facing the massive fountain in the center of the park. It was beautiful and subtly erotic, much like the country itself. The core of the fountain was four carved life-sized women, each facing a compass direction. They were beautiful and posed as water from the fountain sprang from their breasts into a large pool of clean, refreshing, water below. The fountain was a stunning mixture of art and utility and David had spent many moments enjoying the serenity it evoked. On his mind now though, was the decision needed about the C.I.A. Despite his misgivings, there was much to consider still.

So other than feeling foolish at your performance with Ariana, are there any other reasons you don't want to be a case officer? It can't be all seduction ... in fact, I bet it's a very small part of the workload. I didn't enjoy being a sneaky bastard either and it seems a regular need for the career is to pretend to be someone you're not and to keep secrets from those you know and those you love ... but what else? What's on the plus side?

David wanted to be settled in his mind whether he did, or did not, want to pursue a case officer career before he met with Kat. He was thinking maybe not, but he didn't feel he knew for sure yet.

Maybe it's not important if you know before seeing her. Hell, maybe she can help make up your mind. Just go see her. Besides, you don't have to really make up your mind yet. You have one more semester when you get back. There's time.

That was enough for David for now. He rose from the bench and walked the rest of the way to Doña Luisa's. Once there, he looked across the open courtyard and saw Kat at a far table, back to the wall, facing him. She saw him enter and waved. He walked across and sat in a chair next to her.

Kat seemed in a good mood, and she started their conversation.

"Hail the conquering hero!"

David was a bit surprised.

"What do you mean? Is that a little sarcasm? I was a miserable failure. I'll be surprised if the government doesn't want their money back for the hotel room."

This drew a full laugh from Kat.

235

"What are you talking about? You did well young man. Shall we break it down? I'll give you what we saw. And more of what we know about Ariana. The truth is we told you a pack of lies up front … lies of omission. Lies in the sense of what we know and didn't tell you. The lies weren't for any malicious intent, they were just to help us see what we were watching for."

David was hopelessly curious. Kat continued.

"We know that *Daddy Dearest,* Daniel Ortega, is in fact a pedophile and he molested Arianna from when she was age 12, until she was age 17. We know Arianna was crushed when she revealed the abuse and her mother took Ortega's side, publicly disavowing Arianna as a liar. We know Arianna is now living in Costa Rica and is a gay rights activist and that she is a committed lesbian with no interest in men. You didn't stand a chance of seducing her."

David was surprised that he wasn't surprised. It explained a lot. His next thought was that he felt used and foolish for having been hitting on a lesbian. If he had been informed, though, would it have changed his approach? He thought only to the extent he wouldn't have been having thoughts about getting her into bed, but still, he wished he would have known. He felt disgusted with himself at the thought of the extent he had been willing to go to with Arianna.

He met Kat's gaze.

"I need a shower …"

Kat let loose with full-throated laugh.

"I know what you mean. I've had to take a few showers in my career as well. So, how did you do in this context? Quite well actually. You exhibited some fine instincts. Being unobtrusive, pouring out your beers, taking initiative and looking for her in town, and sticking around in character after getting shot down, all things we are looking for in a case officer. So, here's the thing, being a case officer requires two qualities: skill and will. We have established to a certainty you have the skill. It's now simply a matter of whether you have the will, or not."

Kat stopped speaking. David could not yet form his next question. They sat and their silence grew, yet Kat did not seem uncomfortable. She waited. Finally, David spoke.

"So, you're saying it's up to me then, that it's my deciding if I can handle the pressures and focus on the greater good of it as a career?"

Kat beamed.

"Bright boy! Like I've said about you before. The good news is you don't have to decide today. Let it percolate. It may take days, or weeks … possibly even months, but you'll know it with certainty when you do decide. Let's eat!"

Kat dug into her breakfast and David did the same.

He never saw Kat again after that meal. One thing he did take away from their talk however was her advice to not over-think it. He went about his business and enjoyed the remaining weeks of his travels. At the end of it, he wasn't sad.

He had been gone long enough that he was missing home and his folks. He packed up on the last day and walked to the central market where he stepped onto the now familiar *Esmarelda* bus and settled in for the drive to the airport in Guatemala City, and his flight home.

Several months later, on a beautiful spring day, he was back on the campus of Cal State Fullerton. David was walking from a class to the library and was just a week away from final exams and graduation. He wanted to buckle down and study that day, so he stopped at an outside table at the student union and pulled out one of his class folders. He was about to begin reading when he heard a familiar voice.

"David Atwater! … Hello!"

David looked up to confirm, and he smiled.

"Mr. Duncan! I can't say why, but I'm glad to see you."

Jim Duncan smiled and helped himself to a seat across from David.

"I read a glowing report on you from Kat Espinosa a while back. I know you're about done here so I wanted to check in and see what you're thinking about your career options these days."

David was not surprised. Duncan had told him on their first meeting they would talk again when he got back from Guatemala.

"So, you heard about my little adventure with Arianna then. Well, after that, you guys are still interested in me?"

Duncan smiled.

Of course. Kat told you that you did well, yes?"

"Yes, she did. It didn't feel like I did well, but I get what she was saying … If I do choose to become a case officer, don't I have to go through a formal interview or two in Langley?"

Duncan nodded.

"Yes, but truth be told, in the case of many of the college grads we've been interested in, such as yourself, it's a formality. Think about this … for practical purposes, you've been in a three-year interview. If you want the job, it's yours. This really is a decision for you, not us."

David saw the logic of it.

"I have not been thinking about it much until this past week or so. I'm coming close to a decision."

Duncan reached into the pocket of his sport coat and pulled out a card. He handed it to David.

"Do me a small favor. I've led you to the water's edge and there's nothing else for me to do. When you decide, either way, call Mrs. Biondi and let her know if you want to schedule an interview … or not. I understand the complexity of this decision, so take all the time you need."

Duncan stood and extended a hand to David.

"It's been a pleasure, David."

David stood and shook hands with him. As Duncan was walking away, David blurted one last question.

"Mr. Duncan … is it worth it?"

He had to ask the question of the only other *Spook* besides Kat that he knew.

Duncan stopped, turned, and looked at him thoughtful for a moment.

"Think of it as being a candle. It's a way of throwing light into the world, but it consumes you in the process, you're sacrificing a normal life. It's like Heinlein said in *Starship Troopers. Are you willing to put yourself between the desolation of war and those you love?* It really boils down to just that …

240

and there is one other aspect to consider … you should understand it's not all grim. There is a truckload of fun and interesting times to be had along the way. That's the best I can think of to explain what the lifestyle is like."

And with that, Duncan turned and walked away. David was sure this was the strangest advice he had ever been given, and he wanted to ponder it some more. And just like Kat, David never saw Jim Duncan again.

Three days later, David was on a date. It was his fourth date with a lovely girl, Gail. He had met her in one of his history classes and there was no denying they were attracted to each other. They had studied together in a group several times at the campus library, which led to a couple of casual dates and now they were out together having dinner at a Mexican restaurant. He could feel things heating up between them.

They sat, dinner finished, and lingered over their second Margarita. They were talking and enjoying the music as some Mariachis were circulating the floor. The last thing on his mind was the CIA. He listened to Gail talking and he imagined what kind future they might have together.

Gail was gorgeous and confident, with soft curves, hypnotizing eyes, and a sweet, lyrical voice. She could be the one for him, he thought. He could imagine them with a few kids, living a normal life somewhere, happily doing what people do … It had worked for his parents.

He knew she was thinking along the same lines now from a few of her subtle questions earlier that evening.

She was intriguing and he wanted to know her better. While they talked, David's sight was drawn to a small fountain in the courtyard of the restaurant. He compared it to his memory of the beautiful fountain in the central park in Antigua. This one was pitiful in comparison. Then he compared *the women of the fountain* with Gail. The contrast of the statue's cold, erotic, stark beauty in the wider world, to Gail's warm, erotic, familiar beauty in his smaller, known, world.

He listened as Gail talked, but he was also thinking about the question he had asked of Kat all those months ago.

Is it worth it?

He thought about her answer and then about Jim Duncan's answer to the same question. He looked at Gail, meeting her eyes. He held her gaze and reached deep into his heart.

Without intending it, his choice became clear in his mind. It wasn't really a choice of career after all, was it? It was a choice between two, very different, pathways through his life.

He could see one life with Gail, and children, and surety … and he saw the other life, alone, but a life filled with purpose and meaning beyond himself. He saw now that it was not possible to have both. His choices had finally, after months of thought, come down to this.

David's split attention allowed him to give a brief answer to a question from Gail and she continued with her story. David again looked at his choices then, in the flash of a moment, he knew … he knew for sure which path he would take.

He had decided.

A Well Run Dry

Romance ... and love ... from a man's point of view are something of a mystery to many women, men not being known for their proficiency with self-expression for the most part.

Self-expression ... Think of the men you've known ... They run the gamete, don't they? From the John Wayne and Lee Marvin *strong silent types,* to singers, poets, and writers, who after much labor, can get it out there ... as did Shakespeare for example. Who among you ladies didn't have your heart pierced when first hearing William's balcony scene in Romeo & Juliet?

> *But soft, what light through yonder window breaks?*
> *It is the east and Juliet is the sun!*
> *Arise, fair sun, and kill the envious moon,*
> *Who is already sick and pale with grief*
> *That thou her maid art far more fair than she ...*

And so on ... now that's what we're talking about! *Romance* ... never mind how those two star-crossed lovers ended up ... it's beside the point!

As a man, I'll confess much admiration for William's ability to speak directly to the heart of every woman who ever heard him. Most men, I think, would confess they would kill for this ability ... but alas, men are taught rather to soldier on, without complaint or comment. Some of us though push through, at least to a degree.

As for myself? I'm a writer now, no Shakespeare perhaps, but I think I can shed some light ... at least enough for the fair sex to gain an insight or two into the minds of men, so come on in ... and pardon the clutter.

My own journey to true love, and being able finally to express it, has been long. I use a metaphor to describe it ... My journey featured a well.

A water well? ... no ... The well of poetry is what I mean. My journey can be marked with the poetry of inspired romance ... not as refined as William's, but I offer it up anyway.

Mine is a meager well and, after many years, it has indeed run dry. I admire those with the talent for writing well-crafted, inspiring poems, but for me, I've only ever written five, all of which are likely to be judged as awful.

Those of you with more romantic, or forgiving, of natures might give some credit for the feelings evoked, or the visuals chosen ... or for what I thought to be clever metaphors at the time, but you might also still cringe to read them aloud.

I don't care about that now though, as time has shown me it's all okay. The poems were from deep within me when I hoisted them up from my well … in my leaky wooden bucket, with its fraying rope.

Here, years later, when I read them again, I can still feel the thrill that was in my heart when I wrote each one. A small pool of creativity, just deep and cool enough to soothe my soul.

My well was on the edge of a desert however and only a small portion of water was ever to be drawn from it.

All this occurred to me a few days ago as I was sifting through a long-neglected box of old papers and photos. Inside the box were drafts of the five poems, saved and forgotten over the years, and when reading them now, they showed me a pattern threaded through my life.

Each time I fell in love, I was romantic and inspired for a long while and even fancied myself a poet. For some, but not all, of these loves of mine, I was inspired to write some poems.

I love the smell of these old papers and photos by the way. It's a faint, stale, and not altogether pleasant air, but it is earthy, and real … It's my life.

The echoes of that life wash over me as the smell, wafting into my nose, with its molecules of decaying paper, bring me waves of memories and feelings. It has to do with poetry, this nostalgia of mine.

Of the few poems I have written in my life, they've been inspired by a love that I thought would save me. I believed these loves were the reason why I had gone through all my previous experiences, so I could appreciate the one I was with then.

I've been fortunate to have been inspired at those times and I was convinced I was at my last stop with each one.

For those refined folks out there who really get poetry, and tempo, and meter, and whatever else is involved in the formal structures of poems, which mine surely lack, there is one counterweight leveraging mine toward the good, and that is how purely from the heart they were. When written, I had nothing within me but good feelings and good energy … for whatever that may be worth in judging poems.

So where did it come from? This desire to distill my life and feelings into a few lines and package them as prettily as I knew how? To hand them on bending knee to the one who saved me, to the woman of my dreams? … and what of the loves in my life for whom I didn't write poems, who inspired me equally, or even more?

Even though I can't be with any of them anymore, they all touched me and shaped my soul … they made me a much better man than I would have been without having known them.

All these women, the ones for whom I wrote poems, and to the ones I didn't, they are all still a wonder to me.

But this story is about romance … and poetry. So back to why my poems are likely bad.

Why is anyone's poetry bad? There are artists out there … poets who can write about a twig, and it'll make your heart sing with how they describe what they see in it. That's a poet!

I'm more of a plodding type. I'm a plow horse, but I do appreciate beauty when I see a thoroughbred.

When thinking back to the roots of my interests in poetry, I first look to my mother. She had an artistic streak which she never realized. In between her driving us to swim lessons, shopping, cleaning, doing laundry, and a hundred other things, she didn't have much time for her creative side; however, it still leaked out from time to time.

I remember a morning where my brother and I were young. We sat at the kitchen table after she had cooked a breakfast for us. While we ate, she sat at the table with us, and she was writing. I asked her what she was doing, and she told me she was writing a poem. I asked her what a poem was, and she explained poetry to me for the first time.

Years later, after she died, I was going through her box of old papers and photos with my brother … we all have a box of old papers and photos, don't we? … and we found what I'm sure was the poem she was writing that day. The name of the poem was *The Fort,* and it was about my brother, my cousin Sherri, and me … and the first girl I was ever sweet on, our neighbor friend, Denise.

We four kids had converted the crawl space under our house into a *fort* by digging out a shallow pit between a few of the 4 by 4 wood foundation pilings supporting the house. We spread out tarps for ground cover, hung curtains, and brought in candles for light. All very unsafe of course, but that's how it was back then.

The poem was from my mother's perspective, about how it gave her joy to listen to us down there, our four voices carrying up through the heater floor vent in our living room, where she listened, as we had all our secret kid conversations in our private *fort.*

It was a heart-warming experience to read it as an adult.

Something in her poetic nature must have lain dormant in me. An inkling of it appeared when I penned my first *almost poem* in 5th grade – The Chocolate Submarine.

Not really a poem I guess now, but was it a poetic spark? I wrote this *almost poem* for my 5th grade teacher, Mrs. Piper.

It had nothing to do with love though. For me it was about imagination and creativity ... and meeting the requirements of the assignment, to use a list of words she had provided, in sentences, and underline them.

Adverbs? Pronouns? Both? I couldn't tell you the difference even now without looking it up. (To this day I think both my command of spelling and grammar blow, and I thank God for spell check).

At the very least though, this work shows my primitive inclination toward imagery, if not a romantic nature, or the spirit of a poet. It went like this:

The Chocolate Submarine

Everyone has heard of the yellow submarine and nuclear submarines but very few have ever heard the story of the chocolate submarine. It is a very special boat. It can go anywhere and has been everywhere. Anyone can ride on it and nearly everybody wants to ride on it. It can do just about anything and has done almost everything. If someone wanted to take a ride, he must first promise to be true to himself to never look backward and to always have something to work for. Then *the submarine will take you <u>wherever</u> you want to go. <u>Maybe</u>*

you think that the chocolate submarine isn't a real boat but

<u>without</u> it we could never go anyplace. The chocolate submarine

is as real as you think it is.

Mrs. Piper was generous in her grading and her comments, written in her perfect flowing cursive, in blue ink, at the bottom of my returned paper:

"This sounds a bit like philosophy, or a fairy tale – *O."*

In fifth grade an "O" was a big deal. 'O' was for 'Outstanding', the only one I ever got from her, that I recall.

The first romantic poem I recall ever writing was for Wendy. It's remarkable to me that Wendy is the only woman I've known who wrote *me* a poem. By the time I was 25 or 26 I was at least somewhat experienced in romantic relationships, but I had shown no proclivity for poetry until I met her.

She was a beautiful girl who felt in her heart that she wasn't. Of Irish stock, with hypnotic green eyes and shocking red hair, she had the heart of a poetess.

Wendy used to give me small journals, like the kind you buy at Barnes & Noble and never write in ... four inches by six inches, with lined pages ... Wendy wrote in hers though. Hand-written poems ... some her own, some by well-known poets ... and musings of her own, some of which were about me, and how I made her feel, and some more general and philosophical.

The one that touched me most was about an evening we spent together, just sitting in a Jacuzzi at my Stepmom's place, flirting with each other. She wrote this poem and gave it to me in one of her little journals later. I've since lost it, which I regret, but I remember the essence of it. She wrote about how romantic that evening was for her.

I was a little embarrassed at the time because, though it was true I spoke with her about how beautiful the moon was, and how peaceful the water, creating romantic imagery for her ... mostly I was just trying to get laid that night.

And so it goes with young folks. It's hard to separate the inspired fires of spring from plain hormonal over-drive.

I do think her poetic nature influenced me a lot though. Soon after that evening in the Jacuzzi, she and I were in regular company. It was then I wrote the first *romantic* poem I remember ever writing. It was about an afternoon and evening we had spent together the day before. We'd gone out to eat in

Redondo Beach, in California, and we strolled the city pier for a long time afterward, just talking and taking in the sights.

In the poem, I tried evoking some of the things we saw as we walked, and how I felt seeing them with her at my side. I tried to weave these images together to show her what drew me to her … It went like this:

The Pier

Sunset washing the land's western edge,
Fisherman casting cares over ledge,
while watching waves and seagulls' fight.
On this pier, in a trade-wind breeze, a wandering
minstrel offers banjo prophecies, on his stage of cafes, shops,
and neon lights.
Abounding mismatched airs of popcorn, salt-air, and
fish ... drinking in the scene, a couple strolls in bliss.

Their joy akin to kids there seen pulling taffy and kites,
this man ... and muse ... with ginger hair, in a deep blue dress.

She surrounds him now and stirs his breast
While every sight, sound, and smell swirl to his delight.

Her emerald eyes upon him, revealing grace,
Ally with dusk, in smoothing lines from his face.

For him, the world has never been so bright.

No time to despair, for joy so fleet.
Time only to seize these moments complete.

A scarlet ribbon now is left of day,
and somewhere, softly, a saxophone plays.
He knows to seek love is a man's only fight.
She casts a smile upon him, and his heart ignites,
as shape and color fade into twilight ...
He sighs ... and smiles ... and they step into night.

So then ... this was my first effort at writing a poem. Looking at it now, forty some years later, I still get it. I know what the obscure references mean, but does the reader? I wasn't concerned with that then ... or now.

I still see there is a beauty in the poem that I would want to share, if I were a real poet who could re-work it somehow into something breathtaking.

Wendy left me later because I wasn't honest with her.

After this poem, I wasn't inspired to write another for many years. Between the ages of 26 and 58 in fact. I had two wives in there, with six girlfriends squeezed in between, and I didn't write a poem for any of them ... that I can recall.

It wasn't due to any lack of romance or feeling love though.

I was crazy about all of them. I just didn't express those feelings in writing at the time. I guess I can call these *the dry years*. Lots of romance, lots of learning, lots of love … but no writings, no poems … and this is a tale about how men go about *expressing* love, so we'll move on in time.

Of the seven Muses in Greek mythology, the muse of romantic poetry is Erato … and she finally smacked me in the head again one day as my second marriage ended and I too quickly involved myself with Renee. This unexpected reappearance of Erato in my life, after so many years, coincided with my next three relationships.

Oddly, all three of them were former girlfriends, each of whom found me on Facebook. I'll call these years *the Facebook years*.

Renee was another beauty and we found each other for the second time when we were both searching for something lost. When we first saw each other after all those years we picked up like it was the day before, and I was a goner by the end of the weekend.

She made me feel like a man who, dying of thirst, crawls out of the desert to a way station and drinks from a well of sweet, cool water … (I know … another *well* metaphor … what can I say? … it feels right)

In that rush of feelings and emotions, Erato inspired me, and I wrote Renee a very sexy Haiku, which I can't find now, and then a poem, complete with stolen artwork from Bing images.

The poem went like this:

Two souls apart

Leaving her too soon, love forged in fires of youth, not seeing the right of us then as truth.
I left her there under stars, where we watched the waves, with an unspoken knowing in our hearts.
Tears became years, shaping sight to finally see, but she was gone, awing on the winds of destiny. No faith or hope, only time draining on, she became an angel lost to me, without star to chart.
Heavenly grace from the blue … she found me … I know now as part of the grand design.
Late yet, my soul now worthy, with her soul a sweet summer night, we meld and start.

Eyes sunburst and blue, witness to love as grows, two souls become one in each other's sight.

Twin souls bejeweled; hang upon the starry, starry night ... our hearts and souls, never again to part.

Maybe I should be embarrassed? I'm not sure, but I'm not. Despite shamelessly leaning on Van Gogh, and my complete lack of poetic structure, I let love flow from my heart directly onto a piece of paper, and it is what it is.

I still can't find the Haiku I wrote her, but I did write Renee one other short poem.

It went like this:

Across space and time, an Angel found me...amid smoking ruins of life and war.
Without word, her sunburst eyes and fragrant touch soothed my brow...then, bringing me here...to the green and golden fields of Elysium...she healed me.
Across space and time, my Angel found me.

I really did feel like she had saved my life.

I jazzed this poem up for her by pasting it into a serene, Maxwell Parrish-like, PowerPoint slide … I know, quite the romantic devil, aren't I?

Renee left me later because as our passions cooled, as they always do in time, she had no room in her life for the mundane.

Next in the Facebook years was Susan. A stunningly beautiful blond. She was soft spoken, sweet, with a very sharp wit and a thirst for fun. When I had known Susan the first time around, she was one of the girlfriends between wives that I mentioned earlier. Susan was exiting an abusive relationship when I met her, and in the end, that first time around, she couldn't leave him.

Years later, she found me on Facebook, right as Renee was dumping me, and I didn't miss a beat. We talked openly and painfully about what had happened with us before, and what she had done and seen of the world since. We talked about where she was now and where she wanted to be, and we were so in tune that I felt sure she was the one.

By this time, another muse had clubbed me. Calliope, the muse of writing. I wrote a love story about our relationship, that

259

I later shelved. It was so syrupy; it will never see the light of day if I have anything to say about it. I also wrote her a poem. It went like this:

An Angel Seen

A vision I was given fortune to see, once upon my youth
A divine gift, teaching me in God's own way, the natures
of beauty and truth.
She and I, set to meet in a lot of black stone, and broken
glass, and mean ... She came to me instead upon a breezy field
of silver pillars with a lay of green.
Walking my way, waning sun behind, setting ablaze hair
of gold, and a dress of white, bound with flowers, black as night
Drawing near, her grace and beauty flow round me as it
does in the sight of art
Her smiling gaze upon me, paled first the Sun, then in a
moment, too my heart
A haloed muse touched my hand and held me with eyes
of deepest piercing blue.
I was lost to myself for a time, not knowing what to say
or do.
If ever asked in my life, I could never explain how she
came to be with me.

Not knowing how deep her beauty ran even yet, she lifted
herself in affection to me.
With lips soft, and a kiss so sweet, and in an Angel's
voice she simply said 'Hello' to me.
Again, should I be embarrassed? I don't know, but it was from the heart to the pen, direct, when created.

Susan left me later because she was still emotionally unavailable ... and I wasn't.

With timing worthy of an unbelievable movie, my third inspired love during the Facebook years came at the exact moment when I was again adrift, without love.

Liane and I first met when I was married to my second wife. Her husband and I were coworkers at the time, and the four of us became friends for a long while, and we did a lot of socializing together. There was no acknowledgement of any attraction toward each other back then, but it was there, very low key, in the background. Years later, she found me on Facebook. We were both single and it took no time at all for us to get together and fire up a torrid romance.

Now there's this ...

If Renee was a stunning hottie, in a short skirt and a long jacket …

And if Susan was a Southern Belle, with a brain, and charm enough to melt butter …

Then Liane was a biker babe, who paid for law school by being a stripper …

None of these things being exactly true of course, but the images are at least fair illustrations of the contrasts in their temperaments.

Liane was tough. When I knew her before, and later, I most enjoyed watching her deal with stupidity in others. She was always courteous when shredding idiots, but so very, very sweet and open when you got past her wall.

Erato inspired me again and I wrote a poem for her.

It went like this:

Where the Starflower Grows

Scottish Highland bitter cold, yet beautiful with history told

Most venture not there, preferring warmer light and air

I seek it though, as it is where my Starflower grows.

Rapturous bloom, pushing through lichened stone, spread in fullness in warmish noon.

In arctic starlight she folds upon her heart, weathering chill, until in windy day she spreads her art.

262

A surprising beauty in a land so harsh.

Climbing hills, and snow-dusted paths so far, are but nothing to find an earth-bound Star.

Mattering not if seen in day or night; she is in this world, a point of light.

Tough and delicate, transcending time and cold, my heart leaps when her I behold.

Here where my love for the Starflower grows.

So ... for the last time I ask myself, should I be embarrassed? and again, I am not. I poured my soul through my fingertips, onto my keyboard, when I wrote it, and it's me ... It is true ... and I'm pretty sure that poem touched her in some way.

Liane left me later because I was irresponsible, and it scared her.

This, then, brings us to the present.

I'm with Kim now and things are different. I'm where I'm supposed to be ... finally ... and I'm with who I'm supposed to be with ... finally.

I haven't written her a poem yet, but, as with all my
unheralded loves, I've done many other romantic things to tell
her how meaningful she has been in my life.

For me, Poetry has been that well I dug at a way station,
on the edge of the desert. And some water seeped into it …
eventually … when I had dug deep enough, and hard enough, it
produced just enough water to sooth my brow.

Can I dig a little deeper, one more time, for Kim to see if
just one more cup will trickle forth?

It's true that I work under the eyes of another of the
seven Muses now, Calliope, the muse of eloquence. I chase after
her and am a writer of tales, but I don't want to write a story
about Kim just yet … it's too soon … only five years so far.

Calliope will however indulge me, I know, to consult
with Erato one last time, because I want to write my true love a
poem, and hand it to her on bending knee. A good poem if I can,
or at least a serviceable one, and I've figured out how I might do
it.

I bought a copy of the bible for would-be poets
everywhere. *Poetry for Dummies* … I'm reading it now.

And this, ladies, is today's insight into the male brain …
It's not that men don't want to be romantic … its mostly that we

just don't know how to do it expertly, and immediately. It's awkward ... and heaven forbid you see us as awkward. It can't be allowed. It takes a lot of guts for a guy to reach for a skill in front of his love ... it's as bad as stopping to ask for directions for Christ's sake!

But reach I will ... I'll learn what I can from this *Dummies* book, then it's my turn to back Erato into a corner and have her help me structure something beautiful for Kim ... an Opus? If an Opus is a final, masterwork, a herculean best effort, then this will be my Opus. We'll see how my plan works.

Ok ... It's been 12 days ... and it's not working. I read half the book and got bored ... but Erato didn't forsake me. Here it goes, my last ill prepared poem, I am sure, has poured from my heart, onto a page, and it goes like this:

On Solid Ground

How boring! ... How pedestrian ... Is that all you aspire to?
Not asked of me, except by myself ... and I answer, yes.
Suffering tens of years - movies with unhappy ends - seen again
and again. Expecting different outcomes ... But love must be
worthy of trying again, yes? For it's said, 'All you need is love'

In trying again, we age ... and with age comes refinement of
judgment ... and clarity of desire. Love's first rush, so sweet ...
so fleet ... as a butterfly ... is gone too soon. What's left?
Only dreams and desires ... which cannot sustain.
Love is something else then, not what you feel ... learn what it
is, idiot! ... Then you'll be happy!
It takes time ... and much thought ... then understanding comes.
Love is really ... surrendering one's fears.
Trusting one with everything ... because it looks, and fits, and
feels right. I didn't understand this until I met you.
You ...
Meeting online ... What the?!
But there you were ... Non-Smoker ... Master's degree ...
posting a pic of yourself with wet hair and no make-up, standing
on a dock ... SCUBA Queen! ... Cleopatra would approve.
A geographic undesirable, I desired you. I put my best B.S.
forth, and you replied ... but only to say, call me ... I don't have
time to mess around online.
We talked ... and here is where it happened.
Here is where you and I happened.
We talked ...
We agreed to meet ... at Starbucks.
I walked in, knowing you were already there.

You stood waiting for a Mocha Latte ...

framed by a full glass wall ... The sun was low ...

Rays of light circled you, casting a halo on your golden hair.

I joked later a chapel of Angels and Gregorian monks were

chanting around you then.

It's when I knew ...

For you, it took longer.

I could tell you wanted us ... but were cautious none the less.

I was patient, then one day, after you told the neighbors 'No

way he stays' ... my car was still in your drive the next day.

That was your break-through ... you were in ... my break-

through was later ... when you would not let me push you away.

That's what changed me ... I used to want the thrill and energy

... the delight.

Now, all I want is to hear your breath when you sleep, and see

you talk with our pup ... and to listen, as you tell me about your

day, while I try to keep my eyes off your beautiful body ... So, I

look to your beautiful face.

To watch While you move around our place with grace, while I

work hard to keep your pace. I'll never understand how you

came to be, but ... I will always Love you for really loving me.

It took a lifetime, but I learned that love isn't fireworks, or passion, in a burning urn, but it's rather a dove ... sailing the air ... coming to land ... gently ... on a branch ... just above ... the solid ground.

So, that's it then ... my heart is spilled from my body again, and it lays in front of me, one last time, aching to be back in my breast, where it belongs, but I let it sit there ... I watch it for now, not in a hurry, because I'm enjoying the sweet pain of it being out.

There is no more water in the bottom of this well ... my meager, cloudy, pool of poetry ... It has finally run dry.

Not a drop remains, but I feel strangely ... complete.

I'm tossing in the rope now, letting it drop and coil to the bottom of the well. I hear it piling up on top of the rickety wooden bucket below, and I somehow know I'm done with this well.

Kim too will someday let me go, like the others ... but this time, I know, it will be only when I die.